Mary's Terrible Tugboat

"It's true," Mary's mother told her. "Tim actually bought a boat for us today. And you'll never guess what kind! It's a tugboat!"

"That's right," Tim, her new stepfather, said. "One look and I fell in love with the old boat."

A tug boat! What would the girls in the Unicorn Club think? A lot of them had wealthy parents who loved expensive clothes and houses. She had already boasted to her friends about her stepfather, and how he was going to change their lives, how he was going to move them out of this small house into a fancy mansion he was designing, and how his architectural firm built skyscrapers and office buildings.

Just wait until my friends find out we've got a tugboat instead of a yacht, *thought Mary.* Just wait until they find out I've got a handyman for a stepfather!

Bantam Books in the SWEET VALLEY TWINS series
Ask your bookseller for the books you have missed

1. BEST FRIENDS
2. TEACHER'S PET
3. THE HAUNTED HOUSE
4. CHOOSING SIDES
5. SNEAKING OUT
6. THE NEW GIRL
7. THREE'S A CROWD
8. FIRST PLACE
9. AGAINST THE RULES
10. ONE OF THE GANG
11. BURIED TREASURE
12. KEEPING SECRETS
13. STETCHING THE TRUTH
14. TUG OF WAR
15. THE OLDER BOY
16. SECOND BEST
23. CLAIM TO FAME
25. STANDING OUT
26. TAKING CHARGE

27. TEAMWORK
30. PRINCESS ELIZABETH
32. JESSICA ON STAGE
33. ELIZABETH'S NEW HERO
34. JESSICA, THE ROCK STAR
35. AMY'S PEN PAL
36. MARY IS MISSING
37. THE WAR BETWEEN THE TWINS
38. LOIS STRIKES BACK
39. JESSICA AND THE MONEY
    MIX-UP
40. DANNY MEANS TROUBLE
41. THE TWINS GET CAUGHT
42. JESSICA'S SECRET
43. ELIZABETH'S FIRST KISS
44. AMY MOVES IN
45. LUCY TAKES THE REINS
46. MADEMOISELLE JESSICA
47. JESSICA'S NEW LOOK

SWEET VALLEY TWINS SUPER CHILLERS

1. THE CHRISTMAS GHOST
2. THE GHOST IN THE GRAVEYARD

SWEET VALLEY TWINS SUPER EDITIONS

1. THE CLASS TRIP
2. HOLIDAY MISCHIEF
3. THE BIG CAMP SECRET

SWEET VALLEY TWINS

Stretching the Truth

Written by
Jamie Suzanne

Created by
FRANCINE PASCAL

BANTAM BOOKS

TORONTO · NEW YORK · LONDON · SYDNEY · AUCKLAND

RL 4, 008–012

STRETCHING THE TRUTH
A Bantam Book/May 1988
Reprinted 1991

Sweet Valley High and Sweet Valley Twins are
trademarks of Francine Pascal

Conceived by Francine Pascal

Cover art by James Mathewuse

ISBN 0-553-15554-7

Published simultaneously in the United States and Canada

Bantam Books are published by Bantam Books, Inc. Its trademark, consisting of the words "Bantam Books" and the
portrayal of a rooster, is Registered in U.S. Patent and
Trademark Office and in other countries. Marca Registrada.
Bantam Books, Inc., 666 Fifth Avenue, New York, New York
10103.

Printed and bound in Great Britain by
Cox & Wyman Ltd., Reading

To Molly Jessica W. Wenk

One

"I don't care what anyone says," Jessica Wakefield announced, tossing her blond hair. "*Dream Chaser* is positively the best movie in the world!" She challenged her sister Elizabeth to disagree.

Jessica and Elizabeth were identical twins. Facing each other across one of the old-fashioned marble tables in Casey's ice cream parlor, the two girls looked like mirror images. They both had long blond hair, blue-green eyes, and dimples in their left cheeks. But though the pretty sixth graders looked alike, they hardly ever agreed on anything. "I don't know," Elizabeth replied, pausing to sip her root-beer float. "Tom Houston is a good actor, but the plot was completely unbelievable. Everything worked out so perfectly. It wasn't like real life at all."

Jessica loved romance and glamor. She couldn't understand her twin at all. "Oh, Lizzie!" she cried. "Why do you always have to be so practical? That was the most exciting, wonderful movie ever made. Tom Houston is the cutest guy in the universe!" She sighed in tribute to her latest heartthrob. "Honestly,

Lizzie, I don't see why you bother going to the movies at all. If you want to see 'real life,' you could save your money and watch Lois Waller eat three desserts at school everyday!"

"Or Charlie Cashman shooting spitballs," Mary Robinson interrupted. Mary was a seventh grader and a good friend of both twins. With a laugh she squeezed into the booth beside Elizabeth and signaled the waitress. She ordered two Casey's specials. "Lila's joining us," she explained. "She's just calling home to say she'll be late." Lila Fowler was a pretty and popular sixth grader who was Jessica's very best friend in school.

A minute later Lila strolled into Casey's, looking as perfectly groomed as a model. "Hi, you three," she said, sitting next to Jessica. "Wasn't that movie incredible? Tom Houston was gorgeous!"

Jessica gave her twin a triumphant grin. "You see!" she crowed. "Now maybe you'll listen to your baby sister." The twins often joked about Jessica's being born four minutes after Elizabeth. "Everyone in the world except Lizzie knows *Dream Chaser* is a masterpiece!"

"I just wish it had been a more realistic story, that's all. Happy endings like that don't happen to real people."

"They most certainly *do*!" Jessica insisted. "Just look at Mary. She lived in foster homes almost all her life, and just this year she found her own mother."

Like everyone else in Sweet Valley, California,

the Wakefield twins had been thrilled when Mary, separated from her mother as a small child, had been reunited with her.

"And in case you've forgotten, Mary and her mom found each other in our very own living room." Jessica sighed again. "Just like in a fairy tale!"

"It *was* like a dream come true for me," Mary remembered, her eyes shining. "I've never felt so happy."

"Well, that *was* a pretty special adventure," Elizabeth admitted. She smiled at her friend as the waitress brought Mary and Lila's three-scoop specials.

"And Mary's getting happier all the time," Jessica continued, delighted to be proving her point. "Her mom just got married again, and they're all living happily ever after. Aren't you, Mary?"

Mary stared at her ice cream without touching it. "Sure," she said quickly. "We're really happy."

"If your stepfather's so wonderful," Lila asked, "how come I haven't gotten to meet him?" Lila never wasted any time being tactful. "What does he do, anyway?" Lila's face took on a suspicious look.

"He works on houses."

"*My* father owns three houses." Bragging was one of the things Lila Fowler did best. "He also owns a condominium and an apartment building."

"Well, Tim works on houses and apartments, and skyscrapers, too," Mary said, looking flustered. "He's a . . . a sort of architect."

"I knew it!" Jessica looked delighted. "You see, Lizzie? It must be great to have a dad that builds office buildings and skyscrapers."

"My mom would never choose anybody ordinary," Mary insisted again, her voice firm. She paused, staring into Lila's dark eyes. "Tim is very, very special."

"My father is sending me to Europe next summer," Lila said, daring Mary to top her.

Mary looked uncomfortable. She saw Jessica and Elizabeth watching her. "Oh, Tim says Europe is boring," she announced. "He says Africa makes a better vacation." Her eyes shone and a big, broad smile covered her face. "Just before he moved to Sweet Valley, Tim designed a palace for an African king."

"Wow!" Jessica exclaimed. "A palace!" She looked at Mary with admiration. "I guess you must be the happiest person in the world, Mary. You've got just about everything anyone could ask for."

"Except good grades," Mary admitted, frowning. "My report card looks like a national disaster area. Two of my teachers called our house Friday. They want my parents to come in for a conference."

"But, Mary," said Elizabeth, "you've always done so well in school!"

"Well, uh . . . I haven't had much time for homework lately. It just seems like there's always so much else to do."

"I know exactly what you mean," Jessica told

her. "When you have to choose between fun and work, you'd be crazy to choose work. No offense, Lizzie."

Elizabeth laughed. Jessica never *did* see the point of spending time on homework when she could be cheerleading or talking with her friends. But Elizabeth didn't ever feel comfortable until her nightly assignments were completed. "That's OK," she said. "I don't mind being the bookworm in our family." Still, she appeared concerned as she turned back to Mary. "I can't understand why you're having problems doing your work. We used to go all sorts of places together. Lately, though, we've hardly seen you at all."

"Yeah," added Jessica. "Mom asked us about you the other day. She said she hasn't seen you since your mother's wedding."

Mary shifted uncomfortably in her seat. "I just don't have much time anymore. You see, my stepfather always wants to go places with Mom. I mean with Mom and me. So I like to stick around." She looked at Jessica's expectant face. "You wouldn't want me to miss something exciting, would you?"

"Like what?"

"Well . . ." Mary closed her eyes. It was hard to tell what she was thinking. Then she looked straight at Jessica with a big, bright smile. "Like a big dinner out. Tim always wants the three of us to go out to dinner."

"That's nothing," Lila countered. "My dad and I eat out more than we eat in."

"Or shopping," Mary added quickly. "Tim loves to take us shopping and buy me presents."

"He does?" Jessica loved her own father very much. But the idea of a dad who came home every day itching to buy his family presents sounded absolutely terrific.

"Uh, sure. He's bought me so much stuff I can barely fit it all into my room!"

Mary was wearing a great big smile and looking just like a fairy-tale princess. But Elizabeth couldn't help thinking that it sounded too good to be true.

"Wow!" Jessica was thrilled and dying to hear more. "I guess with a stepfather that rich, you won't be staying much longer in that little house your mother rented, huh?"

"No." Mary dipped her spoon slowly into the mound of whipped cream on top of her ice cream. "I mean, of course not. Tim says we're moving to a much bigger house."

"Sure. And how many servants are you going to have?" Lila challenged.

"Well, not any right away." Mary took a bite of the strawberry scoop on her special. "It won't be for quite a while because . . . because Tim is just designing the house now. Naturally, he wants everything just the way Mom and I want it. He's very picky."

"You mean you get to help plan your own house?" Now Lila sounded just the tiniest bit jealous. "Gee, Daddy always moves into houses that are already built. He says it saves time."

"Not Tim," Mary told her. "He likes to take charge of everything himself."

"Oh, great!" Jessica cried. "You should ask for big French doors for your bedroom, with a formal rose garden right outside. And a tennis court," she added.

"Well, I don't know." Mary stopped eating. "I mean, I haven't really thought about it."

"Haven't thought about it! Mary, what is the matter with you?" Jessica rolled her blue-green eyes. "I can see you need someone to help you with this project. How about if I help plan your room?"

"I don't think—"

"First we'll have a big dressing room off the bathroom," Jessica said. "The pool should be right off the rose garden. We'll make it just like the one in *Dream Chaser*."

"Oh, no!" Elizabeth interrupted, exasperated. "Whose house is this, anyway, Jess? Don't you think we should let Mary's stepdad build his own home?"

"And how about a long terrace with a sweeping view of the nine-hole golf course?" Lila suggested.

Mary looked alarmed. "Lila, I really don't think my house is going to be *that* special."

But Jessica and Lila were too carried away to pay any attention. "You'll definitely need a guest cottage," Jessica declared.

"Yes!" agreed Lila. "With its own pool. Something small yet tasteful, full of class. . . ."

"Speaking of class," Elizabeth said to Mary, glad

to change the subject, "are you going to take the jewelry-making classes Mr. Sweeney and Ms. Lacey are giving on Wednesdays?" Even though they had very different interests, the twins had signed up for the after-school jewelry workshop. Lila was also planning to take the course. But Elizabeth hadn't seen Mary's name on the list posted in the main hall. "Ms. Lacey says we're going to start out with silver bracelets!"

"Gee, I'd really like to," said Mary, "but I have to get right home after school."

"Mary, you've just got to come! All the Unicorns have signed up."

"Oh, we were hoping you would come," said Lila. "We're going to make official club bracelets."

Mary, Jessica, and Lila were all members of the Unicorn Club. Elizabeth thought most of the girls in the club were snobs and that the only purpose to their meetings was to talk about boys and clothing. But Jessica loved being a Unicorn more than anything else in the world. The Unicorns were all pretty and popular. They did everything and went everywhere together. And they always wore a lot of purple. Purple was the Unicorn club color. But Mary hadn't been to meetings in quite a while, so she didn't know anything about the club's plans. "Er . . . that's great, Lila. But I still can't come."

Jessica couldn't imagine anyone turning down the chance to make their own jewelry. "You don't have to make the same thing as everyone else, Mary," she explained. "Mr. Sweeney told our art class that you can do anything you want. I'm going to make my bracelet look like two roses twined together. I already did a drawing in class."

"You can't have *that* much homework," Lila insisted.

"I—I can't come," Mary told her, looking very uncomfortable again. "I know just about everybody in school has signed up, and it *does* sound like fun. But I have to get home right after school now. It's the only time I have with Mom all to myself. If I spent it making jewelry or . . . or doing homework, things would never be like they were before."

"What do you mean, 'like they were before'?" Elizabeth asked gently.

"Oh, you know. Before I got a stepfather and Mom got a new husband. It used to be special, just the two of us. Just Mom and me." For an instant Mary's eyes misted over, but then her face broke into a wide grin. "Not that things aren't great now," she insisted. "It's just that I have to give up some things because we're so busy." She set her chin firmly and looked at her three friends with determination. "But I'm *not* going to give up my mom!"

"So that's why you haven't been able to type those articles for us!" Until Mary's stepfather had moved in, Elizabeth, who organized the *Sweet Valley Sixers*, the sixth-grade class paper, had been able to count on her friend to help with the typing. Lately, though, Mary always seemed to have an excuse when Elizabeth asked her for help.

"And that's why you haven't been coming to

the Dairi Burger with the Unicorns?" Jessica asked in surprise.

"I—I've missed being with you," Mary admitted. "But I just can't give up my mom. Things are different now. I hope you understand." She looked at her watch and struggled quickly with her sweater. "Gee, I didn't realize it was so late. I've got to get home. Mom and Tim said they were driving up the coast, but they're probably back by now."

Jessica looked down at Mary's bowl. "But you've hardly touched your ice cream."

"You eat it for me, Jessica." Mary was already headed for the door. "I want to tell Mom all about the movie. See you tomorrow!"

"Boy, Mary sure has changed lately," observed Jessica as she watched their friend race off.

"Yes," Lila agreed. "She's turned into a regular hermit!"

Elizabeth frowned. She missed spending long *Sixers* work sessions with Mary, the two of them typing and laughing for hours on end. "The only thing is, hermits usually *want* to be alone," she told Lila and Jessica. "But I don't really think Mary wants to choose between her family and us." She looked up as Mary slipped out the door. "I wonder why she thinks she has to?"

Two

◇

Jessica and Elizabeth entered the Wakefield home through the sunny, Spanish-tiled kitchen. In his usual position by the open refrigerator, the twins' brother, Steven, was assembling the ingredients for one of his enormous sandwiches.

"Hey, guys!" he greeted them as he pulled a head of lettuce from the crisper. "Guess which mature, sophisticated freshman has been picked to be chairman of the entertainment committee for the next Sweet Valley High dance?" Steven's eyes were twinkling with excitement.

"Today is Sunday, dummy," Jessica reminded him. "How could you get picked on the weekend?"

"Well," he admitted, "the election really isn't until tomorrow. But I talked to Cathy Connors, and she says she's sure everyone's going to want me to be chairman. The whole committee was crazy about my idea of making the dance theme *Dream Chaser*. I want to get a DJ to play all the songs from the movie, and have all the girls dress like Leslie Morgan."

"Ugh!" Jessica looked disgusted. "I didn't like

her clothes at all!" She paused, remembering the movie. "Of course, a room full of Tom Houstons would be wonderful. Your idea's only half bad."

"Thanks a lot," Steven told her sarcastically. "Now, if you two will excuse me, I have some serious work to do." He carried his plate into the family room, where he could watch a football game while he ate his colossal sandwich.

The twins followed Steven, and found Mr. and Mrs. Wakefield already watching the game in the next room. Eyeing Steven's sandwich warily, Mrs. Wakefield commented, "I certainly hope that leaning tower of turkey is more stable than it looks."

"It's ham," Steven corrected. "And it's built to last."

"Sure." Elizabeth giggled. "About as long as anything edible lasts near you—two seconds!"

"You know," said Mr. Wakefield, his brown eyes shining. "I think Steven holds the all-county title in munching out!"

"Hey," Steven protested, laughing with the rest, "what do you mean all-*county*? I defy anyone in the state to make a better sandwich!"

Mrs. Wakefield rolled her eyes and turned to the twins. "How was the movie, you two?"

Jessica sank to the floor with a dreamy expression. "Tom Houston is the ultimate!"

"I suppose that means he's good," her mother guessed.

"Good? He's perfection. He's super. He's—"

"Someone who could use a better movie," Elizabeth finished for her. "Mom, you should have seen how silly this script was. Women threw themselves at him every second, and he never made a single mistake. I mean, you'd think he was playing Superman instead of a race-car driver. He didn't even come close to losing a race in the whole movie!"

"Why should he?" Jessica challenged. "He's not supposed to be an ordinary human, anyway. He's . . . he's . . ." She sighed and waved her hands in the air helplessly. "He's Tom Houston."

"Well, nobody asked me," their father announced, "but I think I agree with Elizabeth. I like to watch stories with which I can identify. And I'm afraid I've made too many mistakes and lost too many battles to identify with perfection!"

"Besides," Elizabeth added thoughtfully, "I'll bet perfection can be pretty hard to live with." She remembered the discussion at Casey's after the movie. "According to Mary, it's nearly impossible!"

Her mother looked concerned. "Elizabeth, what do you mean? I thought everything was going well for the Wallaces."

"For the Wallaces. But maybe not for Mary." Elizabeth remembered how sad Mary's face was when she described her "perfect" stepfather.

"Oh, I'm sure Mr. Wallace will be adopting Mary as soon as it's legally possible," said Mrs. Wakefield. "Then they'll all have the same name."

"Yes," Mr. Wakefield agreed. "These things take

time, but as soon as they've located Mary's real father and made the proper application, they can all become Wallaces."

"That would be great," said Jessica. "After all, Mary can't miss her real father very much. He and her mother got divorced when she was just a tiny kid."

"Yes," admitted Elizabeth. "But don't forget that Mary just found her mother and her real name. I'm not sure she's ready to give all of it up for anyone else."

"That's silly, Liz," Jessica assured her. "Why, with the spectacular house her stepfather is building, everything will be perfect!"

"The Wallaces are moving?" asked Mrs. Wakefield. She had a part-time job as an interior designer and was always interested in finding new clients. "Maybe Andrea would like some help planning her new home."

"Oh, don't worry about that, Mom," said Jessica. "I've already given her lots of good advice."

"I don't think a new house is going to make much difference to Mary," Elizabeth insisted. "There's something really bothering her, Mom. I've asked her over here at least a dozen times in the past month, but she always says no. She never goes anywhere anymore."

"Not even to Unicorn meetings," Jessica added. "We've been operating without our treasurer for weeks now."

"From what I hear," Steve teased, "you don't

have much use for a treasurer anyway. I mean, any club that holds all its meetings at the Dairi Burger has got to be broke!"

"For your information, Steven, Sweet Valley High isn't the only group that can sponsor a dance!" Jessica declared. "It just so happens the Unicorns are planning a big party with a band and everything."

"A band?" Elizabeth sounded surprised. "Do you know how much that will cost?"

"Isn't it fabulous?" Jessica smiled smugly at her twin. "I bet you wish you'd joined the Unicorns after all!"

"And spend my life painting my fingernails purple and gossiping about everyone in school? No thanks." Elizabeth had gone to one Unicorn meeting at the beginning of the year. For her, one was enough. She decided that the Unicorns did nothing but dream up new clothing fads and laugh at girls who didn't follow them. In fact, Jessica and Mary were just about the only two club members Elizabeth respected. "Maybe Mary's just decided she's had enough of the Unicorns."

"No," Jessica insisted. "Mary really loves the club. She's always had lots of fun at meetings, and she comes up with the best fund-raising ideas. Or at least she used to," she corrected herself.

"She *used* to do a lot of things, including spend time visiting her friends." Elizabeth was getting more and more upset, remembering Mary's big, phony smile that afternoon.

"It's true. I haven't seen Mary for weeks," Mrs.

Wakefield said. "I wonder where she's been keeping herself?"

"She just stays home with her mother," said Elizabeth. "She's afraid to let her out of her sight." Elizabeth felt her voice catch a little. "Meanwhile, I feel like I'm losing a friend."

"Hmmm. I haven't talked to her mother in a few weeks. Maybe I'll give her a call and see how things are going."

Elizabeth felt much better. Mrs. Wakefield had a knack for fixing things. She had been the one who helped Mary's mother find a job so she could stay in Sweet Valley. "Gee, thanks, Mom. It just seems like Mary's problems are bigger than she can handle."

"Well," Jessica observed, "if having a stepfather who's going to build her a mansion with a pool and tennis court is a problem, I wish I had some problems of my own!"

Elizabeth remembered the way her twin had taken charge of Mary's future home. "Jessica, you were so busy building that house yourself, you didn't let Mary get a word in edgewise."

"Well, somebody had to get excited about it, didn't they? All you and Mary wanted to do was sit around and mope about her grades!"

"Grades? Is Mary having trouble in school, too?" Mrs. Wakefield asked, looking concerned.

Elizabeth hadn't wanted to mention how badly Mary was doing in school, but now that Jessica had let it slip, it seemed important to explain things. "You know how terrific Mary's grades have always been, Mom. I just know something is bothering her. I mean, if her new stepfather is so wonderful and everything is going so well, why is Mary afraid to leave her mother's side—even to do homework?"

"I'm not sure, Elizabeth." Mrs. Wakefield exchanged glances with her husband. "But I'm going to try to find out."

Three

◇

"Hi, Mom. Has the carpet come yet?" Mary rushed into the living room of the small, cozy house Mrs. Robinson had rented when she got a job in Sweet Valley. It was Monday, and Mary's classmates were eating lunch in the school cafeteria, but she'd remembered that her mother had taken off work today. Mary was sure she would have her mom all to herself without her stepfather around. She stopped short when she saw the slender, bearded man in the kitchen. "Hello, Tim," she said slowly. "What are you doing here?"

Tim Wallace smiled and joined them in the living room. "I live here, remember?"

Mary remembered, all right. She also remembered what it had been like before her stepfather moved in. After years of hoping, after nights filled with tears and prayers, she had found her mother at last. At last she didn't need to be jealous of her friends. She no longer looked at their mothers, wishing she was their little girl, too. She had a real mother of her very own. For a short time, anyway.

She watched her new stepfather circle her mother's waist with his broad arm. She watched him pull her close to him. And worst of all, she watched her mother smile up at him, looking as though he was everything she needed. Maybe he was. Maybe they didn't need her at all. Maybe she was just in the way.

"I thought Tim was working on a house today," Mary whispered to her mother. "I thought you were going to be home alone, Mom."

Mrs. Wallace hugged her daughter. "I thought so, too, honey. But it seems I've got two terrific friends who decided to visit me while I wait for our new dining room carpet." She smiled again at Tim, who now put his arm around Mary, too. But Mary stepped away, ducking from under his hand. She didn't feel like being part of a threesome.

"Actually, I just came back for a minute," Tim explained, stopping to retrieve a battered guitar case from under the couch. "I wanted to tell your mom about my big purchase."

Mrs. Robinson smiled with enthusiasm. "Oh, yes, Mary. Wait'll you hear what Tim bought this morning!" She led Mary to the couch and sat down beside her. "Come on, Tim, sing her the song you wrote about our new boat!"

Tim sat down on the other side of Mary, his old guitar in his lap. Mary looked at them in disbelief. "Our new *what*?" she asked.

Tim smiled at her, but Mary was sure it was only to please her mother. "You've just become part owner of a magnificent ocean-going vessel, young lady." He winked at Mary, but her expression made it clear she wasn't at all interested in what he had to say. "And," he continued, "in honor of this occasion, I've just composed a suitable song!"

Mary had heard enough of her new stepfather's songs—especially the sticky-sweet love songs he was always singing to her mom. Every time Tim took out his guitar, Mary's mother looked at him with a shy, loving smile that made Mary feel more left out than ever.

"It's true," Mary's mother told her. "Tim actually bought a boat for us today. And you'll never guess what kind!" She looked as proud and happy as Mary had ever seen her. "It's a tugboat! You know how Tim's been working on refinishing a kitchen for that family over on Bellevue Drive? Well, it turns out the father used to work at a naval shipyard. He's had this old boat for years and years."

"That's right," Tim said, strumming a few chords. "He liked the work I did on his house so much, he said he'd love to see me try my hand at restoring the tug. One look and I fell in love with the old boat." He laughed and then began to sing a silly song called "I Think I Can," about a decrepit old boat. The boat got into a race with a sleek yacht, and in the last verse chugged its way to victory.

When the song was over, Mrs. Wallace clapped loudly. She thought her new husband a very talented musician. "Oh, Tim, you're wonderful! Mary and I are so lucky to have you in our family. Right, Mary?"

Mary didn't answer. She pulled closer to her mother on the couch, holding her hand tighter than ever. Her stepfather's voice was pleasant to listen to, but his song had made her lonely and frightened.

"It'll take time to fix the old tug up, but it's something we could all do together—a real family project." Tim smiled hopefully.

Mary felt them both looking at her. She knew they expected her to be pleased with their big surprise. But it was just one more thing she'd been left out of. They'd been talking about it, planning it together. It wasn't really hers at all. And having a tugboat was pretty embarrassing. In Sweet Valley almost every other family owned a sailboat or a cabin cruiser. Why did her new stepfather go and buy some leaky old boat?

"Yep! A chance like this doesn't come along too often." Tim was beaming, his arm again around his wife. "I haven't seen a tug like this since I was a kid."

A tugboat! What would the girls in the Unicorn Club think? A lot of them had wealthy parents who loved expensive clothes and houses. She had already boasted to her friends about her stepfather and how he was going to change their lives. How he was going to move them out of this small house into a fancy mansion he was designing. How his architectural firm built skyscrapers and office buildings.

"Of course, the sanding and painting will take time," Tim continued. "And it'll be hard work!"

"Won't it be fun?" A shadow crossed her

mother's pretty face as she looked at Mary. "It'll really be something when we've got it all fixed up!"

"Something" is right, thought Mary. *Just wait until my friends find out we've got a tugboat instead of a yacht. Just wait until they find out I've got a handyman for a stepfather!* She knew she should have felt guilty about saying that Tim built houses instead of fixed them. But actually, it had been sort of fun to talk about a glamorous, make-believe stepfather instead of the person who was trying to take her mother away. And maybe what she'd said wasn't a lie anyway. Maybe her *real* father was more than an ordinary carpenter. Maybe he was like the fathers of the girls she'd met in Sweet Valley; he might be a doctor, a lawyer, a banker—anything by now. If only her parents hadn't gotten divorced when she was a baby. If only she didn't have to get used to a brand-new father who just pretended to like her to please her mother!

"Your mother and I decided that you should name our boat, Mary. What do you think we should call her?" Tim asked.

But Mary couldn't stop thinking how much better things used to be. If only they had stayed the same. If only her mother were still Andrea Robinson instead of Andrea Wallace. Now she didn't even have the same name as her mother. She didn't feel like part of this new family at all. "Why don't we call the dumb boat just what it is," she said angrily. Bolting from the couch, she ran upstairs toward her room. "A rotten wreck!" she shouted. Quickly, before they could see the tears streaming down her cheeks, Mary disappeared into her room.

At first Mary tried not to listen to the voices in the living room below. But soon, as the conversation drifted up to her, she found herself straining to catch the words. "I don't know what's come over her," she heard her mother tell Tim. Her voice was tired and sad. "Mary never acts like this, Tim. I just don't know what to think anymore. She's changed so much. I feel like I hardly know her."

"That's according to *you*." Tim, too, sounded tired. "Ever since I've known her, though, Mary hasn't changed at all. She's still doing poorly in school, she's still angry at the world. And she still doesn't seem to like me at all!"

"Please, Tim, be patient with her. It takes time to get used to big changes like the ones we've been through. I know the two of you will get along together if you just give her a chance."

"There's nothing I want more than for us to be a real family, honey. But I'm afraid you have things a little mixed up." Tim started to walk across the room. "If this thing is ever going to work, it's *Mary* who has to give *me* a chance."

"She will. I know she will." Now Mary could hear her mother following her stepfather to the front door. She covered her ears with her pillow, but she could picture Tim kissing her mother good-bye before he hurried out the door to his next job.

When she was absolutely certain that Tim had left, Mary dried her eyes and went downstairs.

"I'm afraid we didn't have much of a lunchtime together, sweetheart," her mother told her.

"We never have any time together anymore," Mary complained. "Alone, I mean."

"We have lots of time to be mother and daughter, Mary. We've got the rest of our lives. My loving Tim doesn't change that at all."

"But it does. Don't you see?" Mary wanted to make her mother understand just how much everything had changed. At first the idea of her mother getting married had seemed exciting. The two of them had picked out dresses for the ceremony and talked about plans for the honeymoon trip. But then her mother and Tim had left her alone with the Altmans, the foster family she'd lived with before she'd found her mother. It was only for two weeks, but each night she woke up tossing and crying, convinced that she'd lost her mother once more.

"What I do see, young lady, is that it's time for you to get back to school, and you haven't eaten a thing." Quickly Mrs. Wallace grabbed an apple and some slices of cheese and slipped them into a plastic bag.

Mary was glad that Jessica and Elizabeth had not been able to come to her mother's wedding. They had had to cancel at the last minute. At least she didn't have to introduce them to Tim. If only her mother would send him away. If only she could put everything back the way it used to be. Just the two of them. No handyman for a stepfather, no broken-down boat, no crying in bed while Tim and her mother whispered downstairs.

"Here, silly," her mother was saying as she put a twist tie around the bag of fruit and cheese and handed it to Mary. "Maybe you can sneak a bite or two in between classes."

Mary looked sullenly at the bag. Her mother never used to forget about making her lunch. Mary dropped the bag on the counter. "I'm not hungry," she said, then scooped up her books and headed for the door. "I lost my appetite!" She slammed the door behind her, glad that for once she'd forced her mother to think about her instead of Tim.

Four

◇

Janet Howell, the Unicorn Club president, was furious as she scanned the faces around the cafeteria table. "I scheduled this meeting at lunchtime just so Mary could be here. This is the fourth meeting in a row she's missed." A bossy eighth grader, Janet wasn't used to club members skipping meetings. She liked to think that the Unicorns were the most important thing in the whole middle school—in fact, in the whole world. "Does anyone know where she is?"

Sitting at the end of the table next to Lila, Jessica raised her hand. She had seen Mary in the hall just before lunchtime. "Mary went home," Jessica told Janet. "She needed to talk to her mother. I'm sure it was important."

Janet frowned. "Well, how can we have a meeting about fund-raising without our treasurer?" She glanced around the table again. Everyone was still eating.

At the end of the table Lila groaned. "Look, Janet," she spoke up. "It's not exactly a federal offense to miss a few meetings." Lila was Janet's first cousin and one of the few Unicorns who ever stood up to her.

"I think Mary has shown she's not ready to be a club officer," Janet replied.

"The way she runs this club," Lila whispered to Jessica, "you'd think it was the United Nations or something!"

"Well, all I know," Jessica whispered back, "is if this meeting isn't a short one, I'm going to be in a lot more trouble than Mary. I've got math next period, and if I show up without my homework one more time, Ms. Wyler is going to kill me!"

"You are pushing Wyler to her limits," agreed Lila. "Last week, when you were passing notes to Helen Bradley, she got so angry I thought her eyes were going to pop out of her head!"

As Jessica and Lila laughed, Janet banged her fork on a cafeteria tray as if she were a judge in a courtroom. "This meeting had better come to order," she announced, glaring at the two sixth graders, "or we'll never find out how much money we need to raise for our big party next month."

Kimberly Haver, a seventh grader, raised her hand. "Janet," she said, "we don't need Mary to tell us we have no money left in the Unicorn treasury."

"That's for sure," agreed Tamara Chase, another seventh grader. "We used all our money for those purple sweatshirts we bought for the club."

"I've got a great idea," Betsy Gordon piped up. "And it won't cost us a cent. Why don't we let my brother's high school band play for our party? He says they need the practice. I bet they'd play for free."

Jessica sighed loudly, and some of the other girls put their hands up to their mouths to hide their smiles. Everyone knew how horrible Johnny Gordon and the Waves sounded. "We'd be better off with no music at all," Jessica whispered to Lila.

"Uh, thanks, Betsy," said Janet. "But I think we need something different for this party. My bunkmate from camp, Judy Walker, is coming to visit me, and I already told her we're sponsoring a dance. Anyway, Judy is president of a club at her school. They call themselves the Shooting Stars and they give really terrific dances all the time."

"How about a singer?" asked Lila. "We need a really dreamy singer for our party."

"Yeah!" Ellen Riteman, another friend of Jessica's, agreed. Her brown eyes flashed, and her voice got high and excited. "Lila's absolutely right. Why, if we had a romantic singer, we might get boys to dance more."

"How about someone who knows the songs from *Dream Chaser*?" Jessica suggested. "That's what the high school is planning for its next dance." Jessica gave a knowing smile. The Unicorns always like to be filled in on what the older kids were doing.

"That's a terrific idea, Jessica," exclaimed Kimberly. "Do you think we could give the party at your house, by the pool, Lila?"

Lila's pool was, without a doubt, the biggest,

most luxurious swimming pool in all of Sweet Valley. "Sure," she agreed readily. "Daddy won't care." Mr. Fowler was usually so busy traveling on business that he let Lila do just about anything she wanted.

"This is dreamy!" Ellen declared. "I'm going to dress just like Leslie Morgan."

"Well, *I'm* going to dress a lot better than that!" Jessica assured them. "I'm going to wear my blue sundress with the beige jacket. And my new Unicorn bracelet. We're bound to have finished them by then."

"Me, too." Soon everyone was planning their outfits and discussing decorations. But Jessica had still another surprise planned.

"I just might have a very special dance partner, too," she said in a mysterious voice.

"Who?"

"Oh, just Tom Houston, that's who."

"Are you kidding, Jessica?" Ellen stopped describing Leslie Morgan's gold lamé jumpsuit and stared at her friend in astonishment.

"Well, I've been writing to him every week, and he's even sent me a photo."

"Is this photo 'personally signed,' just like the one you got from Johnny Buck?" Janet asked, sounding very superior. She hadn't forgotten the time Jessica boasted to everyone that the famous rock star had autographed a photo just for her. It had turned out that the picture had been signed with a rubber stamp and passed out to a concert crowd with hundreds of identical photos.

"Not everyone is as caring and wonderful as Tom Houston," Jessica replied haughtily. "I'm going to write him and tell him about our club's *Dream Chaser* party. I'm going to ask him if he'll sing the theme song for us."

"He'd never come in a million years!" Betsy Gordon exclaimed. But her expression showed that she hoped he would.

"Maybe not," Jessica told her coolly. "But it never hurts to try." She was sure all the Unicorns, especially Janet, would be incredibly impressed if she could get Tom Houston to come to the party. Why, Janet might even put her in charge of the whole dance.

"Well," concluded Kimberly, "if we're going to count on Tom Houston to entertain, we might just as well give up the idea of a party."

"What?" Janet declared. "And let the Unicorns be shown up by the Shooting Stars?" She wasn't about to let her friend from camp laugh at her or her club. "Let's let Jessica try." She smiled hopefully at Jessica. "I nominate Jessica Wakefield for chairman of our entertainment committee. All in favor, raise their hands."

Jessica's heart started to pound as all the hands at the table went up. What would she do if Tom Houston turned her down? She smiled confidently and decided to worry about that later. "What about decorations?" she asked Janet.

Janet frowned again. "Hmm . . . I don't think we have any money for decorations." She sighed.

"And speaking of money, I think we'd better elect a replacement for Mary. In fact, I'm not so sure Mary even deserves to be a Unicorn."

"Oh, come on!" Lila whispered just loud enough so Janet could hear her.

"After all," Janet went on, ignoring her cousin, "if she's not responsible enough to attend meetings, why should she be in our club at all?"

Jessica was furious, but she didn't dare challenge Janet. Janet was too popular and important to cross. Still, it wasn't fair to push Mary out of the club when she wasn't even there to defend herself. Jessica poked Lila in the ribs. "Janet's your cousin," she whispered. "Do something!"

"Why not give Mary one more chance?" Lila asked. "After all, she did most of the work typing up the celebrity cookbooks."

Janet looked around the table. It was clear that most of the girls agreed with Lila. "All right," she conceded. "We'll continue this meeting after school at the Dairi Burger. But if Mary's not there, she's out of the club." She tapped her pencil impatiently on the tray. "This meeting of the Unicorns is now adjourned."

As the club members were getting up from the table and piling up their empty trays, Jessica looked toward the other end of the wide, windowed cafeteria. Thank goodness—Elizabeth was still there! She raced over to tell her twin about Janet's ultimatum.

Elizabeth and three of her friends—Amy Sutton, Julie Porter, and Sophia Rizzo, were planning the next issue of the *Sweet Valley Sixers*. Munching on the last bites of their sandwiches, they reviewed the latest student council news, discussed the poetry column, and wondered how they were possibly going to get everything into print before next week.

The four girls stopped talking when they saw the expression on Jessica's face. "What's wrong, Jess?" asked Elizabeth.

Jessica poured out the story of the Unicorn meeting. Even though Elizabeth didn't have much use for the Unicorns, Jessica was sure she understood how much the club meant to Mary. "We've got to talk to her before the end of school today," she explained. "If we don't get her to that meeting at the Dairi Burger this afternoon, Mary will be out of the club." Jessica shuddered, thinking about it. "She'll be a total reject!"

"Speaking for all us non-Unicorns," Julie Porter replied, "I think things could be worse, Jessica!"

"Oh, sure," Jessica said apologetically. "But not for someone like Mary. She likes to be popular and have fun and do neat stuff."

"I think you just made us feel worse," commented Amy.

Sophia smiled. She understood best of all what Jessica was trying to say. Before Elizabeth had befriended her, Sophia had known just what it was like to feel left out. "I think Jessica's right," she said. "Mary needs the Unicorns just like we need each other."

"How can Janet be so ridiculous?" Elizabeth said. "It sounds so unfair!"

"Well, you know how bossy Janet can be," said Jessica.

"Does anyone know what classes Mary has this afternoon?" asked Julie.

"Sure," said Jessica. "Elizabeth and I have history class, and there's a seventh-grade science section right across the hall. I always wave to Mary during class."

"OK, Jess. I guess we're the ones to tell Mary." A frown knit Elizabeth's brow. "But you know how she is lately. She'll probably want to rush right home."

"Not this time. Not if I tell her she's going to be kicked out of the Unicorns," said Jessica.

"I guess you're right," Elizabeth agreed. She stood up to take her tray to the front of the room. "The rest of you keep an eye out for her, too. Mary's had enough changes in her life lately. She sure doesn't need to become an ex-Unicorn!"

Five

Jessica and Elizabeth were relieved when they saw Mary walk out of the room across the hall from history class. Elizabeth winked at her twin as Jessica got up from her seat and scooped up her books.

"And just where do you think you are going, Miss Wakefield?" Mr. Nydick asked sarcastically as Jessica headed for the door.

"But the bell rang, Mr. Nydick." Jessica looked around, embarrassed to see that the rest of the class was still seated. "Isn't class over?"

"You're right on one count." Mr. Nydick smiled as Jessica sank back into her seat. "The bell *has* rung. But I'm afraid your teacher hasn't quite finished talking." He rubbed his chin, then ran one hand through his gray hair. "Now, let's see . . . where was I?"

Jessica felt desperate. Mr. Nydick almost never kept his students after the bell. Why did he have to turn into a chatterbox today of all days?

". . . Oh, yes. I was going over your assignment for tomorrow. The real builder of the Roman Empire was Augustus. . . ."

Would he ever stop talking? Jessica turned in her seat and caught Elizabeth's eye. She pointed out the door to where they could both see Mary. She had stopped to talk to a girl in the hallway just outside Mr. Nydick's room. Jessica waved and tried to signal to her, but Mary didn't see.

"So, I want you to list as many of Augustus's accomplishments as you can, but I'd like you to write a detailed paragraph on your favorite one." Mr. Nydick watched Jessica waving, and frowned. "Would you like to invite your friend in for a refresher course, Miss Wakefield?" Blushing crimson, Jessica stopped signaling Mary and shook her head. With the whole class watching, she sighed quietly and faced the front of the room.

"All right, then. I'm not asking for a polished essay. Just your thoughts on one of the great Augustan triumphs." Again he stared at Jessica. "Is that clear?"

"Oh, yes, sir!" Jessica sat up straight, looking bright and eager.

When Mr. Nydick dismissed the class, Jessica darted into the hall and looked left and right. She caught sight of her tall, blond friend leaving the building. "Mary! Mary!" she shouted, and hurried after her, clutching her books in one hand and waving frantically with the other. "Wait up!"

But Mary didn't look back. Just as she ran through the front doors, Jessica collided with Bruce Patman and Rick Hunter, two seventh graders who were standing at the top of the steps with their arms full of oaktag posters. The three of them and a pile of books and cardboard ended up in confused heaps all over the stairs.

"Hey! What's the hurry?" The two boys stood up and helped Jessica to her feet.

"Next time you decide to rush a guy, give him some warning, will you?" Bruce Patman smiled at Jessica.

Jessica thought Bruce was the most gorgeous boy in the whole middle school. "Sorry," she said. "I was so anxious to get to our Unicorn meeting, I wasn't watching where I was going."

Rick was the seventh-grade class president, and though much quieter than Bruce, he was just as cute. "Are you all right?" he asked, looking a little worried.

"Sure," Jessica assured him, delighted to be talking to the two most popular boys in the school. "Gee," she said, turning her brightest smile on them, "I guess you never saw anyone so clumsy."

"Well," Bruce replied quickly, "if that accident was just a trick to get us to ask you to help us with these posters, it worked."

"Yeah," added Rick, stooping to retrieve the big cardboard sheets that lay scattered around them. "We could use some help. Mr. Sweeney wants us to hang them all over."

"I'd like to," Jessica replied. "But I really have to get to a meeting." She looked worriedly toward the path where she'd seen Mary just a minute before. She wasn't anywhere in sight.

"Well, if we don't want a lot of kids showing up at the wrong jewelry classes, I guess we'd better get started," Rick said to Bruce. The two boys started back toward the building.

"What do you mean?" Jessica asked, chasing after them. "What are those posters?"

"Sign-up sheets," Bruce told her. "The jewelry class next week is so crowded they had to add extra sections."

Jessica lowered her eyelashes. "Are *you* taking the class, Bruce?"

"I sure am. My mom's birthday is coming up and I thought maybe I could make something for her."

"That's so thoughtful," Jessica cooed. "What are you making her?"

"I thought a silver charm for a necklace might be neat," Bruce suggested.

"What a fabulous idea! I love charms. Maybe I could help."

"Great! Let's make sure to sign up for the same class. I was going to make a big silver letter P. What do you think?"

"I think you had better stop gabbing, Jessica, or we'll miss the Unicorn meeting," Lila Fowler interjected, coming up to them. "Did you forget about it?" Lila's father didn't get along with Bruce's father, so Lila thought a lot less of Bruce than Jessica did. "Come on. Let's get going."

"OK," Jessica agreed, waving at Bruce and heading down the steps with her friend. "I already told Bruce and Rick I couldn't help."

"Rick Hunter?" Lila stopped at the bottom step and turned to see Rick stapling a poster onto a bulletin board. "Why didn't you say so?" Lila didn't think much of Bruce, but Rick Hunter was an entirely different matter! The shy, popular boy had a way with everybody, and besides being handsome, he was one of the best tennis players in the school. Lila loved tennis, and she liked flirting, too.

Lila quickly headed back up the steps to join Rick and Bruce. Jessica followed frantically behind her. "Wait a minute, Lila. We don't have time for that now. We have to find Mary and tell her about the meeting."

"Don't be such a party pooper," Lila scolded. "The meeting's not until three-thirty. We've got plenty of time." Her long brown ponytail swished from side to side as she strode up the stairs. "Oh, Rick, do you need help?"

While Lila held posters, Rick stapled them. Jessica knew that her friend expected Bruce and her to form another team. Still, she couldn't help thinking about poor Mary. After a few minutes she tapped Lila's shoulder and told her she wanted to speak to her alone.

"You can stay if you want to," she said when they'd walked around the corner from the boys. "But I have to go look for Mary."

"Don't you dare leave me alone!" Lila's brown eyes blazed. "That would make everything look too obvious. Jessica Wakefield, if you walk away now, I'll never speak to you again."

Even though Lila was her best friend, Jessica knew that she could carry grudges forever. She also knew better than to cross Lila when she was determined. So the four of them worked together for half an hour, replacing all the old signup sheets with the new posters. Stapling the last board in place, Rick announced, "I guess that does it." He smiled easily and effortlessly, the way he did at everyone, but Lila seemed to think it was just for her. "Thanks a lot. If there's anything we can do in return, just let us know."

"There is," Lila told him, giving Jessica a knowing glance. "Walk us to the Dairi Burger. You could probably use a sundae after all that work."

Jessica was practically floating by the time they approached the Dairi Burger. She couldn't wait to see the Unicorns' faces when she and Lila walked in with the two most popular boys in school! But as they entered the popular after-school hangout, Bruce asked a question that brought Jessica quickly down to earth. "So, what's this special emergency session all about, anyway?" he said.

Jessica stopped short just inside the door. Oh, no! Mary! Because of Lila they'd never gotten the chance to catch up with Mary. Now, if her friend didn't come to the meeting, she'd be out of the Unicorns. *And it would be all my fault*, Jessica thought. Frantic, she surveyed the crowded room. She saw Ellen Riteman sitting at a table with Kimberly Haver and Tamara Chase. She saw Janet and two of her eighth-grade friends at the table across from them. But she didn't see Mary anywhere.

Just then Bruce spotted some friends across the room. "OK, girls," he said, "see you two later." Before Rick could say a word, Bruce had grabbed him by the elbow and led him toward his friends, leaving Lila and Jessica alone at the door.

What a mess! They hadn't found Mary, and Bruce and Rick had walked off so quickly that none of the Unicorns had seen them together. Jessica followed Lila dejectedly toward Ellen's table, but then the door opened behind them and a familiar voice stopped Jessica in her tracks.

"Jessica! Lila! Wait up." Mary, panting, rushed up to her friends. Her face looked anxious and worried. "Has the meeting started yet?"

Jessica sighed with relief. "Boy, am I glad to see you! How did you find out about the meeting?"

"Elizabeth stopped me on the way home and told me all about Janet. Thanks for spreading the word, Jessica."

Jessica never let an opportunity pass to take credit for something. "No problem. What are friends for?" she said breezily, then steered Mary to the two tables where the others sat. "Look who's here!" she announced cheerfully.

"Mary! Are we glad to see you," Kimberly told her.

"We thought you'd forgotten all about us," added Ellen.

"Of course I haven't," Mary told them. "It's just

that I've been really busy." She helped Jessica and Lila bring up extra chairs, and the three girls squeezed in to form a tight circle around one of the Unicorn tables.

"So what have you been up to?" asked Ellen. "We haven't seen you in ages!"

"She's been having an incredible time," Jessica answered excitedly. "Her stepfather is handsome and rich and he's building them a brand new house."

Mary felt embarrassed. Maybe she'd been carrying her boasting too far. "We're not moving yet, Jessica," she cautioned. "But we have been keeping pretty busy. Tim has all kinds of new projects. Today we bought a boat."

"A boat!" Kimberly exclaimed. "That's fabulous! Is it a yacht?"

"Uh . . . kind of. I mean it might not be *that* big. I haven't even seen it yet."

"Can we all go for a ride?" Jessica could picture herself on board a luxurious yacht, her hair streaming in the wind.

"Gee, I guess so." Mary was glad her friends still wanted to be with her. But how would they feel if they knew Tim was only a carpenter? What if they found out her "yacht" was really a tugboat? She wasn't at all sure they would feel the same way about her if she told them the truth. She wasn't sure about anything anymore.

"Attention, everyone." Janet banged on a table

with her spoon. "I think everyone knows why I've called this special meeting," she said, glancing at Mary. "I hope that we can finally have our treasurer's report."

Mary stood up quickly. "I'm afraid I really can't be of much help, Janet," she announced. "If we're going to hire a band with the money in our treasury, we're going to have to find one that will work for three dollars and ten cents!"

The girls at both tables looked dejected. "That won't even pay for decorations," said Jessica.

"I'm sorry. But we spent just about everything on our club sweatshirts."

"Are you absolutely sure that's all the money we have?" asked Janet. "I mean, you *have* been away a lot lately, Mary. Maybe there's something you left out."

"I'm sure," Mary replied. "I double-checked the figures."

"And that's not all the bad news," Lila added. "I called home after lunch today. The housekeeper says Daddy's put the pool off-limits until the filter's fixed."

"Oh, no!" Ellen cried. "You mean we can't have the party at your house?"

Lila nodded sadly.

"Oh, Mary, I just wish your stepfather would hurry up and finish your new house," said Kimberly. "It would be perfect!"

Mary looked embarrassed. "I'm afraid it won't

be ready for a long time," she insisted. "I . . . told you how picky Tim is."

"It's going to be terrific," Jessica told the Unicorns. "It's going to have a swimming pool and tennis courts and—"

"Maybe not all that terrific," interrupted Mary quickly. "It's just a new house." It wasn't exactly a lie, she told herself. After all, Tim *did* keep talking about buying the house they were renting and adding on a couple of rooms. "It'll be just like new," he was always saying.

"Well, what about a fund-raiser?" Janet suggested. "Do you think we could raise enough by next month, Mary?"

"Maybe. We'd have to work really hard, though. If not, we couldn't possibly—" A shocked expression passed over Mary's face and she stopped talking. She stared at the entrance to the Dairi Burger. "Oh, no!" she gasped. The other girls looked up to see Mary's mother and a thin, bearded man walk through the door.

Smiling when they spotted Mary and the Unicorns, Mrs. Wallace and Tim walked straight to the tables where the girls were gathered.

"Hello, darling." Mary's mother was beaming with pleasure. "What a nice surprise! What are you doing here?"

Mary wanted to sink into the floor. She wanted to go to sleep and not wake up for a million years. "I was just going to ask you the same thing," she told her mother, wishing that Elizabeth hadn't found her and that she'd missed the club meeting after all. As Jessica and the other girls gathered around to meet her new stepfather, Mary wished she'd never joined the Unicorns at all.

Six

Mary stared at her mother and stepfather in disbelief. How could they have appeared in the Dairi Burger, of all places? "I thought you were going out to dinner," she told them.

"We were," Tim explained. "But we hadn't driven two miles before your mother got a craving for a chocolate shake." He winked at the girls clustered eagerly around them. "So here we are. Sorry if we crashed your party."

"It's not a party, Mr. Wallace," Jessica told him. "It's a Unicorn meeting."

"A what?" Tim looked confused.

"I'll explain everything on the way." Mary was already on her feet, easing away from the table. "As long as you're here, we may as well all go out and eat together."

"All right, honey," her mother agreed. "Let me just order our shakes and we'll take them with us." She turned toward the counter at the back of the room. "Why don't you introduce your friends to Tim? I'll be right back."

Now Mary looked plainly miserable. "Tim," she said in a voice that was barely audible, "these are my friends Jessica, Lila, Ellen, and Tamara." She gulped as she saw Janet and the other Unicorns approach her table. "They're all members of our club." She remained standing, but her stepfather pulled up a chair and joined the group at the table.

"Hello, girls," he said agreeably. "I'm glad to meet some of Mary's friends."

"Oh, Mr. Wallace," Jessica told him, "we've heard all about the exciting work you do." She smiled charmingly. "I'd love to hear about your latest skyscraper."

Tim look confused. "I'm not sure what you mean, Jessica. The last job I had was in an apartment house, but I wouldn't call it a skyscraper."

Mary felt dizzy and faint, and thought her whole world was about to collapse around her.

"Have you named your new boat yet?" Ellen asked eagerly. "How many people does it sleep?"

Now Mary's stepfather laughed. "Well, the sleeping quarters aren't exactly luxurious, but it looks as if she had a working crew of about six."

"A crew?" Tamara was impressed. "Your boat must be the biggest one in Sweet Valley!"

"Can you tell us all about the summer palace?" Tamara piped in, eyes shining with admiration.

"Ohh!" Mary suddenly doubled up and collapsed into a chair. She looked very pale and held her stomach. "Ohhh!"

Mrs. Wallace was at her daughter's side in an instant. "Mary, what's wrong?" she cried.

Mary was pale and trembling as she struggled to her feet. "I feel awful," she told her mother. "Really sick."

Tim looked at his wife, then stood up. "I think we'd better get you home right away, young lady," he told Mary. "Jessica, Lila, all of you—it was nice to meet you, and I hope you'll come visit us soon."

"We'd love to," Jessica replied enthusiastically. "We haven't visited Mary in ages." Not, she realized, since Tim had appeared on the scene. "Hope you feel better, Mary."

Holding tight to her mother's arm, Mary looked terribly frightened and unhappy. "I'll be OK," she said. "Just as soon as I get home and into bed." She smiled weakly up at her mother and clutched herself still tighter. As the three of them left the Dairi Burger, Tim reached out to pat Mary's back. But she shook off his hand and shrank still closer to her mother.

Mary felt better as soon as they were safely in the car. But Mrs. Wallace was too worried about her daughter to go straight home without a stop at their family's doctor. Tim drove the car past the turnoff for their house and took them to Dr. Costa's office.

"What are we doing here?" Mary asked. She had been almost lulled to sleep as she lay against her mother's shoulder, and was surprised to see the doctor's familiar parking lot.

"I don't want to take any chances with my only

daughter." Mrs. Wallace laughed. "You've been acting strange lately, anyway. I think it's time for a checkup."

It didn't take Dr. Costa long to determine that Mary was as healthy as could be. In just a few minutes she was sent outside to the waiting room while the doctor, her mother, and stepfather had a discussion.

But she couldn't resist trying to listen to the words that drifted from the doctor's office. "It's not easy," she heard Dr. Costa say, "to deal with as many life changes as Mary has had to confront recently. Have there been any other problems?"

Mary couldn't hear everything they said, but she heard enough to convince her that her mother and Tim were telling the doctor the same things they'd said to each other that afternoon. Mary heard her mother mention the two teachers who called to schedule a conference about her poor grades, and she heard Tim describe the way she constantly rejected his affection and how discouraged he had become.

"I don't have any magic formula for you," Dr. Costa said a few minutes later. "But I can tell you one thing. That child needs to feel she counts in this new family of yours. She needs to be reassured that no one's taken her place. I've been seeing Mary since she first moved in with her foster family," he continued. "The Altmans are fine people, but for Mary there was only one person who mattered in her life: her mother. You can't expect that to change overnight, Tim. You have to let Mary find out for herself that there's enough room in her heart for you, too."

Mary thought it strange to hear Dr. Costa talking about her being able to accept Tim, when all along she'd been worrying about Tim accepting her. Maybe things *were* partly her fault. Maybe Tim really did care about her.

The phone was ringing when the three arrived home. It was Jessica, calling to find out how Mary was feeling. Anxious to make sure her mother and Tim didn't hear the conversation, Mary took the call on the upstairs phone. That gave her mother and Tim a chance to have a conversation that Mary didn't overhear. If she had, she might have felt better about her stepfather's feelings toward her.

"You know, honey," Tim said to his wife when Mary was safely upstairs. "I think the doctor's right. Mary *is* afraid I'll take you away from her. That's why she doesn't like us being alone together and why she won't leave your side."

"There must be some way we can make her feel needed and special, Tim. I know that's all she wants."

"What about her birthday?" Tim said softly. "That's coming up in a few weeks. Maybe we could give a big party. You know, invite all her friends and show her how important she is to us?"

"Oh, Tim! That's perfect!" Mrs. Wallace declared.

"And I've got a better idea still," Tim said proudly. "While you were getting our shakes at the

Dairi Burger, Mary's friends were pumping me for information about our new boat. It seems Mary's already told them all about the tug." He shook his head. "Boy, from her reaction earlier today, I never would have guessed she was so proud of it. Anyway, why don't we have the party on the boat?"

"Great!" Mrs. Wallace's eyes were shining with enthusiasm. "We can fix up the boat secretly in the next few weeks. I'll put up lots of decorations. Oh, Tim, she'll be thrilled!"

But when Mary walked into the living room from upstairs, she didn't look thrilled at all. "What are you two whispering about?" she asked sourly. Once again it seemed as if the two of them were leaving her out of things.

"Oh, nothing at all," her mother sang out, squeezing Tim's hand happily.

Just a minute ago, when she was sick, her mother had been cuddling her, Mary thought. Now she was paying attention only to Tim.

"Don't you have homework, honey?" Mrs. Wallace said, winking at Tim.

"Not really," Mary said grumpily. She wasn't going to leave them alone again, to whisper and plan things without her. "Besides, I feel sick again."

Her mother reached over to feel Mary's forehead. She stroked her daughter's hair and pulled her against her.

Smiling, Mary watched Tim get up from the couch and go upstairs. "Oh, my head," she moaned into her mother's shoulder, snuggling closer.

"I thought it was your stomach that was bothering you before."

"It was. But now my head hurts, too." Mary felt safe and warm cradled in her mother's arm. It would be perfect just to stay there, cozy and content. Even if she never did homework for the rest of her life, even if she failed every course and lost all of her friends, it would be better than losing her mother again.

Tim came downstairs, his arms loaded with Mary's schoolbooks. "Here you go," he said, handing her the textbooks and her spiral pads. "I thought maybe as long as you weren't feeling well, you and your mother could work on your homework together right here on the couch."

Tim smiled kindly, then left the room. "Well," Mary admitted, looking cautiously at her mother, "maybe I *do* have a little homework I could do."

"OK," Mrs. Wallace told Mary, tucking an afghan around Mary's legs. "Why don't I make us some tea, and we'll start working."

Mary sank back into the plump sofa cushions, the fuzzy blanket snug around her. For a sick girl with tons of homework, she felt pretty wonderful!

Seven

◇

"Dear Mr. Houston," Jessica wrote in her huge, loop-filled script. She studied the pink sheet of stationery in front of her and frowned. Then she crumpled the sheet and tossed it into her wastebasket. She took out her fourth sheet and wrote, "Dear Tom—"

"Hi. How'd the Unicorn meeting go?" Elizabeth poked her head out of the bathroom that separated the twins' bedrooms. "Is Mary still in the club?"

"She sure is. Everything's fine. Except for my writer's block. I need help, Lizzie."

Elizabeth frowned. "If you're going to ask me to do your homework for you again, Jess, I'm afraid you're our of luck. I just came from a *Sweet Valley Sixers* meeting and I have a ton of homework of my own to worry about. I just wanted to find out how Mary did."

Jessica glanced back at the letter. The 'T' in Tom looked all wrong. She'd have to start another sheet. "Well, you don't have to worry about Mary. And Lizzie, you'll never guess who came in for some shakes while we were having our meeting. . . ." She paused dramatically. "Mr. and Mrs. Wallace, that's who!"

Elizabeth laughed. "And what's the handsome prince like? Did he ride into the Dairi Burger on a white horse?"

"No, but he's really cute, and Mary told us he's just bought a new boat. It has a crew, and it must be the biggest boat in the marina. We're all going to go for a ride on it!"

"Well, I guess everything's all right then," Elizabeth said, not sounding too convinced. "I'm glad I saw Mary before she went home. Why didn't you catch her after English, Jess?"

"I bumped into Bruce Patman, and by the time I had helped him put up posters for the jewelry class, Mary had already left. Honest, Liz, I really tried. It's just that Bruce needed help. And after all, he's so—"

"Conceited and obnoxious," Elizabeth finished for her. "He thinks he has the right to tell everyone what to do. Next time you've just got to stand up to that bully."

"Oh, I will, Liz, I promise," Jessica said, her eyes wide. "Oh, and speaking of promises," she said, changing the subject. "I told Janet Howell I'd write this letter to Tom Houston. I really could use some help."

"Why are you writing to Tom Houston?" Elizabeth moved a pink mohair sweater and a pair of jeans from the corner of Jessica's bed and sat down.

"Well," Jessica began. "I just thought that if I wrote, I mean if *we* wrote him a really impressive, desperate letter, he might agree to sing at our Unicorn party."

"You must be kidding, Jess!" Elizabeth exclaimed. "What makes you think a famous movie star like Tom Houston has time to come to the Unicorns' party?"

Jessica looked timidly at her sister. "The way you write, Lizzie, I just know you could talk anybody into anything!" She sat down on the bed beside her twin, the pink paper and a pen in her hand.

Jessica's flattery didn't faze Elizabeth one bit. This time Jessica was asking for the impossible. "First of all, Jess," she said, "even William Shakespeare couldn't convince Tom Houston into taking a night off to come to your party! Second of all, I have a ton of homework to do. And last of all, Amy and Sophia are coming over after dinner to do some more work on the newspaper."

But Jessica wasn't about to give up. "That's terrific," she said as Elizabeth got up and started back to her room. "Amy and Sophia are almost as good at writing as you are. Among the three of you we should come up with a great letter to Tom!"

Elizabeth shook her head and closed her door. She sat down at her desk and settled down to work. She had written the first paragraph of her social studies assignment when the bathroom door opened.

"Lizzie, you know that absolutely darling skirt you got at the mall last week?" Jessica said in her sweetest voice.

Elizabeth sighed. She knew she was in for a battle. "You mean the one Mom bought for me, the one I haven't worn yet?" she asked.

"I was just thinking how perfect it would look with my apricot-colored top," Jessica observed. "I was working on that horrible English assignment Mr. Bowman gave us, when I started to think about the awful clothes he wears. You know, how everything he puts on either clashes or is at least ten years out of style?"

Elizabeth laughed. "And Mr. Bowman's wardrobe made you think of mine?" she asked, teasing.

"Well, in a way. I thought about the jewelry classes next week and about how I wanted to look good because Bruce and I are going to work together on a charm for his mother. I thought about how I'd positively die if I had to wear something everyone had already seen. I mean, I'd be as pathetic as Mr. Bowman!"

Elizabeth looked through the bathroom door at the piles of clothes strewn all over her twin's room. Jessica loved clothes—*new* clothes. She tired of something as soon as she'd worn it, and even though her drawers and closets were crammed with sweaters and skirts and dresses, she always complained that she had nothing to wear. "I do not consider Bruce Patman any reason to have you working in my brand-new skirt, Jessica," she scolded. "For your information, jewelry-making isn't a tea party. Ms. Lacey says we're supposed to bring smocks because the solder and glue get all over everything."

"I can't believe it," Jessica wailed. "My own sister wants me to look like a nerd while I'm working right next to Bruce Patman!" She collapsed onto her sister's bed.

"Here," Elizabeth offered, determined to get some homework done before dinner. "Why don't you wear that top with my denim skirt? That way you'll be wearing something you've never worn before, without getting my new outfit spoiled." She strode to her closet and found the skirt.

"Well . . . " Jessica began, getting up. "I guess I *could* wear that, *if* you and your friends help me with the letter to Tom Houston."

Elizabeth picked up the ruffled pillow from her corduroy bedspread, took careful aim, and threw it just as her twin slammed shut the bathroom door. She was still laughing when her mother called up the stairs.

"Dinner, you two! I need some help with the table."

When the twins came downstairs to the dining room, Mrs. Wakefield said, "We'll only be three tonight. Your father and brother went to the basketball game at the University."

"Great! That means we don't have to listen to Steven being a pain," Jessica commented as she helped set the table. "I think his mouth is growing even bigger than he is!"

Mrs. Wakefield laughed. "You know as well as I do, you and your sister thrive on your brother's sarcasm. I don't know what the three of you would do without one another to pick on!"

"We'd probably have a very peaceful dinner." Jessica sat down and peered into the vegetable dish. "Hmmm," she said. "My favorite, mashed potatoes!"

"I'm glad you like it." Mrs. Wakefield smiled. "I made enough food for tomorrow night, too. I have a meeting with a design client, so you'll all be on your own."

Elizabeth was already ladling gravy over her pot roast. "I don't think we'll be suffering, Mom," she said approvingly.

"I don't think a certain friend of yours is, either," said Mrs. Wakefield. "I spoke with Mrs. Wallace about Mary today."

"Maybe I was wrong to worry, Mom. Jessica met Mary's stepfather today, and she said he was terrific."

Her mother nodded. "I got the same report from Andrea. And even though she may be slightly prejudiced, I *do* think the Wallaces are doing everything they can to help Mary adjust. They're even giving her a surprise birthday party on their new boat."

"They are?" Jessica and Elizabeth looked at each other. They both loved parties, especially surprise ones.

"Yes, indeed. I had a long talk with Mary's mother. It seems that she and Tim are really worried about her, too, Elizabeth. But I think they've decided that she just needs time to get used to her new family. And they hope this special birthday will show Mary and her friends how much they care about her."

"Wow!" Jessica was ecstatic. "Wait till I tell the Unicorns!" She leapt from the table but got only a few steps before her mother called her back to her seat.

"I think we should let the Wallaces give out their own invitations, don't you? Andrea wants to call Mary's friends. And, of course, she'll be calling all the Unicorns. It sounds like quite a big party!"

"It sounds like quite a boat," exclaimed Jessica. "Oh, I can hardly wait. I wonder if I should wear my blue blouse or my green boat-neck sweater."

"I wonder if you're going to eat some of my pot roast," added her mother. "You haven't had a bite since I mentioned the party."

"I'm too excited to eat." Jessica stared at her sister's empty plate. "Lizzie, I swear you don't have a romantic bone in your body. How can you eat at a time like this?"

"I can eat *Mom's* pot roast any time!" Elizabeth stood to take her plate into the kitchen. "Come on, Jess, it's time to clean up."

"I can't do dishes now," Jessica complained, following her sister reluctantly to the sink. "I just polished my nails before dinner."

"Fine," said Elizabeth. "I'll rinse, and you load the dishwasher."

"But I have a million calls to make," Jessica protested.

"You heard what Mom said," Elizabeth warned. "Don't breathe a word about the party. Especially to Mary."

"Oh, Lizzie, you never trust me to keep a secret. You should know I won't breathe a single, solitary word of this to anyone except Lila. And Ellen. After all, they're my best friends besides you." With that she rushed off toward the phone.

Elizabeth sighed. "When it comes to secrets," she said softly to herself, "those two are about as good as taking an ad out in the newspaper. Pretty soon everyone will know about Mary's surprise."

Eight

◇

"Personally," announced Lila, who was eating with Jessica and Tamara at the Unicorn table in the cafeteria, "I think a yacht party would be the perfect setting for some dancing. Besides, Mrs. Wallace told Jessica's mom there's going to be music." It had only been a few days since she'd found out about Mary's surprise party, but Jessica had already let nearly everyone at school in on the secret. "I'm just glad Mary's in the seventh grade," Lila continued. "That means Rick Hunter will be at the party. It's going to be just perfect—the waves gently rocking the boat, and me, dancing in Rick's arms!"

"Aren't you rushing things a bit, Lila?" asked Jessica. "None of us has even been invited yet."

"But you said she's calling next week. I wonder if I should wear a sundress or a jumpsuit."

"Wouldn't it be fun if the Unicorns all wore the same thing?" asked Tamara, who loved to start fads. "We could get white pants to go with our purple sweatshirts."

"Yeah!" exclaimed Jessica. "And we could all get

some dangly earrings and wear our club bracelets. After all, we should look our best for such a fabulous party. Besides," she added, glancing across the cafeteria to where a group of seventh-grade boys were joking loudly, "if Mary's whole class is invited, that means Bruce Patman will be there, too."

"Hey!" said Tamara. "I've got a great idea. Why don't we walk over to the mall after school and look for outfits for the party?"

"All right," Lila agreed. "Daddy's off on another trip, and I can't wait to spend some of the money he left me! Let's tell everyone in the club, and we'll all meet outside after school, and we'll—"

All three girls looked up as Mary walked toward them, her lunch tray in hand. They all stopped talking at once.

Mary wondered what was going on. Why had all her friends been whispering behind her back? She decided to pretend she hadn't noticed. "Hi," she said. "Want to go to the Dairi Burger after school?" She slipped into a chair beside Jessica. "Mom and Tim are going out to the harbor this afternoon, and I don't feel like going." In fact, she'd wanted to go with them, but they had rushed off without her.

"Uh . . . gee, Mary," Tamara said, "we sort of had other plans." She shrugged and looked at Lila and Jessica.

"That's OK," Mary said. "We don't have to go to the Dairi Burger. I'll do whatever you want."

Jessica didn't want to hurt Mary's feelings. But even though the party was still two weeks off, she was sure that if the girls didn't get to town that very afternoon, they'd never get to the mall to find earrings for the party. "Well . . . that is, we aren't doing anything special. Nothing nearly as neat as going on your new boat."

Mary couldn't understand why everyone was trying to get rid of her. Earlier that morning her mother and Tim had acted just like Jessica was now. They had gotten very quiet as soon as she came in sight, and refused to tell her why they wanted to race off to the harbor after work. When she had asked to tag along, Tim shook his head. "I think it's time you spent some time with your friends from school, young lady," he'd announced, sounding as if he thought he was her real father.

"Boy," she told Jessica, picking up her hamburger. "If I hear any more about that dumb boat, I'm going to be seasick before I ever get on board. Which I'm beginning to hope is never." She wished everyone would stop talking about the boat. She was afraid they would find out the truth.

Just then a thought occurred to Mary. Maybe they'd already figured out that the "yacht" was nothing more than a battered tugboat. Everywhere Mary went all week long, groups of girls were talking and whispering, but as soon as she tried to join in, they always stopped. Maybe they were all laughing at her behind her back.

"Anyway," she said, "I'd choose you guys over that silly boat any day. So what do you say? Let's do something together."

"Sure. OK," Jessica promised her. "It's just that we were planning, that is, we—"

"Actually, Mary, we were going to work on our designs for the jewelry class after school," Lila interrupted. She knew that Mary hadn't signed up for the workshop.

"Yes!" Tamara and Jessica smiled at each other with relief.

"Don't forget," Tamara reminded Jessica between bites, "classes start at the end of this week, and we want to make sure our club bracelet is the best ever."

"Gee," Jessica said, "Elizabeth loves horses, and she's pretty good at drawing. Maybe I could ask her to sketch a pattern we could trace. Unicorns are just horses with horns, aren't they?"

"Don't let Janet hear you say that!" Mary said, laughing.

"Well, I really need a pattern I can trace. I'm not very artistic," said Jessica. She leaned into the group of girls. "I'm actually going to be working on two jewelry projects," she whispered.

"You are?" Tamara looked curious.

Jessica smiled proudly, but she tried to sound as if she weren't too excited. "Yes. Bruce asked me to help him work on a charm for his mother," she explained casually. "He even fixed it so we're in the same class."

"Wow!" Tamara exclaimed. "Lucky you!"

"I'm kind of sorry I never signed up," Mary admitted. "It's just that Mom and I have started doing my homework together, and I don't want her to feel that I'm letting her down. After that conference she had with my teachers, she's really worried about my grades." Mary didn't have to think about Tim so much anymore. He always made a point of leaving the two of them alone on the couch while Mary reviewed all her assignments with her mom. He'd even started building a desk that would fold out from the living room bookcase so she could work downstairs.

"Well, while you're all making your bracelets, I guess I'd better get busy and try to dream up some way of raising money for our party." She stood up, placing her napkin and empty plate on her tray.

As the other girls got up with their trays and headed for the door, Jessica looked smug. "Well, at least we don't have to worry about entertainment for the dance," she told Mary. "Tom Houston would have to be the biggest jerk in the world to turn down the letter Elizabeth and Amy Sutton helped me write the other night."

The three girls stopped walking and gathered around Jessica. "Is it really good?" asked Mary.

"Good?" Jessica laughed. "I cried while I was writing it down. It's brilliant!"

"You don't really think Tom Houston is going to come to Sweet Valley and sing for us, do you?" Lila looked as if she'd never heard anything so silly in her life!

But Jessica refused to be discouraged. "Just you wait, Lila. I want to see the look on your face when

Tom walks into our dance." Jessica had only mailed the letter that morning, but already she could picture her triumph when Tom Houston appeared. "He'll see me from across the room," she said, her voice soft and dreamy. "Then he'll rush over, take my hand, and say, 'Jessica, I've been dying to meet you.'"

Lila put her hand to her stomach and laughed. "Come on, everyone, let's run to the girls' room before class. I think I'm going to be sick!"

"Tom," cooed Jessica, ignoring her friend's teasing, "I've been waiting to meet you, too. I'm so *glad* you could come." She left the cafeteria with the others, walking down the hall as if she were floating.

"Jessica!" Elizabeth raced up to her twin. "I must have called you three times, Jess. What are you thinking about?"

"It's who, not what," corrected Mary. She laughed, and she and Jessica stopped to talk to Elizabeth while Lila and Tamara waved and hurried off down the hall to class. "Jessica has a lot of faith in your letter to Tom Houston. She's already rehearsing for his visit!"

Elizabeth smiled. "I wouldn't count on anything, Jess," she warned. "Movie stars are pretty busy people."

"No one could be too busy to read *that* letter, Lizzie. You're the greatest writer that ever lived."

"Thanks, Jess. But that's not going to help me get the *Sixers* out on time. We've been writing all week, but now we have so many articles, it looks like it will take another week to type them all." She sighed and readjusted the books in her arms. "I was just on my way to ask Amy and Sophia to stay after school again."

"I'm free after school Elizabeth," Mary put in. "I'd be glad to help."

"That's terrific, Mary," Elizabeth said gratefully. "I didn't even ask you because I figured you'd want to get home quickly."

"Not today. I'll meet you in Mr. Bowman's office after school."

"What a relief! The way *you* type, we'll be done in no time. Thanks a lot."

Mary didn't mind at all. In fact, she was delighted to find someone who didn't want to get rid of her or rush her off somewhere. At the end of school she raced to join Elizabeth and her staff in Mr. Bowman's classroom. She'd been so used to rushing home that she'd forgotten how good it felt to be with friends. "Let's get to work," she suggested eagerly when she found everyone gathered around the old mimeograph machine.

"Too late," Sophia announced happily as she and the others watched Mr. Bowman crank out the first copies of the front page. "Mr. Bowman beat us to it."

Mr. Bowman looked up and smiled. "I took pity on my poor editor here," he said, putting his arm around Elizabeth. "She's been complaining all week, so I went ahead and got Ms. Carey's typing class to work on the articles last period. They're all done, and the presses are rolling."

"Oh." Mary knew she sounded disappointed, but she'd been looking forward to helping Elizabeth. "That's good."

"Hey!" Amy grabbed a copy of the front page as it rolled off into the tray. "Look at our lead article! Doesn't it look great?"

Mary studied the page. Across the top in big, bold letters ran a headline: SIXTH GRADE TO LOSE CLASS PRESIDENT. She didn't understand. "Isn't Linda Lloyd doing a good job?" Linda had been elected their class president in the beginning of the year, and so far everyone Mary knew thought she was doing just fine.

"Oh, she's been a terrific president," Julie Porter explained. "It's just that her family is moving away. Caroline Pearce, our gossip columnist, got the scoop when Linda told her at lunch last week."

"Hey, why don't you run for president, Elizabeth?" Amy suggested. "I think you'd make a really great class officer."

"Me?" Elizabeth was surprised by Amy's idea. But she loved to plan and organize; maybe being the sixth-grade president would be fun. "I don't know," she mused.

"That does it!" announced Mr. Bowman, joining them with a huge stack of papers in his arms. "Who's ready to distribute the latest news?"

Elizabeth, Julie, Sophia, and Amy groaned. The girls loved to write *Sixers*, but none of them enjoyed collating and handing out the paper. Mary volunteered eagerly, though. "Oh, come on. I'll help, and we'll get finished in no time!"

"Now there's the kind of spirit I like to see!" Mr. Bowman laughed and handed her the stack. "Ms. Robinson, I hereby appoint you chairman of our collating committee."

"Thanks again, Mary," Elizabeth told her. "When we're finished here, I think we all deserve a reward at Casey's Place. What do you say to four chocolate shakes?" She paused and smiled back at Mr. Bowman. "Or five," she added, "if you want to come, too."

Mr. Bowman shook his head quickly. "No thanks," he told her. "I tried visiting that hangout one day last year. As soon as I walked in, every boy and girl in the whole place stopped talking at once." He shook his head again. "I don't think a teacher is anyone's idea of after-school fun!"

In half an hour the girls had sorted and stapled all the copies of the newspaper. After distributing them to each homeroom, they were out the door and on their way to Casey's Place.

"Why did you invite Mr. Bowman?" Amy asked Elizabeth. "You know he always turns us down."

"I know," Elizabeth replied, laughing. "I just didn't want him to feel left out."

"Yeah," Mary agreed, falling quickly into place beside the other girls. She remembered how she'd caught the Unicorns whispering behind her back, and how Tim and her mother had rushed off and left her behind. "Being left out is no fun at all."

Nine

◇

"Oh, Lizzie, I wish you and I were in the same jewelry class. I could sure use your help." Jessica, rummaging through her closet, had thrown most of its contents onto her pink shag rug. Dresses, skirts, and blouses lay everywhere.

Watching from the safety of the bathroom doorway, Elizabeth giggled as the tornado of clothes blew across her twin's room. "I don't need to be in your group to tell you what you should wear to work with Bruce Patman. I know for a fact that green is his favorite color—money green."

"Very funny, big sister, very funny." Jessica took several steps back and surveyed the piles of clothes on her floor. Then she scooped up a pink-and-white print blouse and paired it with the blue slacks she found hanging from the doorknob of her closet. Then she carried both to the full-length mirror on the bathroom door. "But I wasn't even going to ask you about clothes. It's about the surprise present I'm making for Mary."

Jessica, concentrating on her image in the mirror, didn't see the look of surprise on her twin's face. "What present?" asked Elizabeth.

"A Unicorn bracelet, of course. Mary didn't sign up for the course, so she's bound to feel awful when everyone shows up at her party wearing their club bracelets." She tossed her blond hair, judging the effect of the pink blouse against her tanned face. "I wanted to make it extra special. Sort of a sign that we all are really glad she's our friend."

"Gee, Jess. That's a great idea."

"Well, what do you think? Does this pink wash out my face?"

"I think it looks terrific," Elizabeth told her truthfully. "It's you."

"I know," Jessica said, frowning, "but I'm afraid it might be Kimberly, too." She threw the blouse back into the pile on the floor. "She wore a blouse almost exactly like it last week. I'd die if anyone thought I bought this after I saw hers!"

Elizabeth groaned. "Well," she said. "I'll leave the wardrobe problem for you to solve by yourself. But I'd love to help with Mary's gift." She watched Jessica make her way through the pile of clothes and sit, Indian-style, on her bed. "What did you have in mind?"

Jessica cleared a space on the bed beside her and patted it, inviting her twin to sit next to her. "I'm going to engrave her name on it and everything. And that's where I need your help, Lizzie."

Elizabeth sat down on the space Jessica had cleared. "But your engraving is much prettier than mine," she insisted. She pushed more clothes out of the way so she could lie down on her side and prop herself up.

"Well, remember the pattern you drew, so we could all have the same unicorn on our bracelets?" In the first class, Jessica had traced her unicorn onto her bracelet and used the engraving tool to cut the picture into the silver band. "I've traced it onto Mary's bracelet, too. But I wanted to do something special with her name. I wanted to put roses around it. You know, like the ones you drew for your bracelet?"

"That *would* be pretty," Elizabeth agreed. "Let's get some paper, and I'll make a sketch." She stood up and started looking in the drawers of Jessica's desk. She pulled out three chocolate bars, a bag of potato chips, and finally a tablet of drawing paper. "Boy," she remarked. "I guess you never have to worry about being sent to your room without dinner!"

"When you hate homework as much as I do, Lizzie, you need all the energy you can get." Jessica turned serious. "Do you really think she'll like it?"

"She'll love it. It's a perfect present!"

"Of course, it'll be from both of us. I mean, since you're doing the drawing and measuring her wrist."

Elizabeth sat back down on the bed. "I'm *what*?"

"Measuring her wrist," Jessica repeated. "I need to know what size to make it." She paused thoughtfully. "Mary's thin, but she's taller than we are. I need to be sure I'm not making her bracelet too small."

"Jessica, don't you remember when Mary gave you her bracelet to wear, before she found out that her real mother had given it to her? We don't have to measure her wrist. We already know," Elizabeth said, excitedly.

The twins worked on drawings until dinner and then, after Elizabeth had finished her homework and Jessica had complained about hers, they did some more sketches. "I think the one with the flowers around the Y is just right," Jessica said as Elizabeth was brushing her teeth in the bathroom. "This is going to be the best surprise ever!" She lay back in bed and flicked off the light on her nightstand. "Mary's mother called everyone in the club today. Our invitations are official!"

"I'll bet she had no idea we've all known about the party for a week." Elizabeth giggled. "For once, Jessica, your gossiping didn't make a bit of difference."

"I know," Jessica answered contentedly. "Mary doesn't suspect a thing!"

Mary had become more and more suspicious as time went on. All week long no one had been able to see her approaching without looking suddenly uncomfortable. Girls who had been talking happily stopped as soon as Mary came into view. "Hi," Mary would say casually, pretending not to feel hurt and lonely. Then she would walk away, wondering what was wrong.

At home things were even worse. Tim and her mother never stayed around when she returned from school. Instead of the homework sessions with her mother she had begun to count on, Mary found herself alone with nothing to do. Her mother suddenly seemed to think the boat was more important than her grades.

"Why can't I come with you?" she asked her mother every day for over a week. "Tim said we were all going to work on the boat together."

"Oh, we will, dear," her mother assured her. "It's just that Tim and I want to get the dirty work out of the way first. We wouldn't want you to get hurt."

But the way she and Tim smiled and whispered each time they set off for the harbor didn't make what they were doing seem dangerous. It was all an excuse, Mary thought angrily. Just a way for them to get away. They didn't want to be with her, after all. Nobody did. Except for Elizabeth.

The next day when Mary got to school, she was greeted by Elizabeth right away. "I have something important to ask you," Elizabeth said eagerly. "Can you meet me for lunch, or do you have to go home?"

Mary was only too glad to eat lunch with someone besides the Unicorns. Lately all they'd done was whisper rudely in front of her. They were always mentioning some kind of secret party, and it was quite clear that Mary wasn't included in their plans. "Sure," she told Elizabeth. "Hey, why don't you come have lunch at my house? Mom won't be home or anything, but it would be fun not to have to eat cafeteria food."

What she really meant was that she'd love to get away from school; where she didn't seem to fit in anymore. She smiled with relief when Elizabeth agreed to walk home with her at lunchtime.

"What a terrific little desk!" Elizabeth said later, when they'd walked into the Wallaces' living room. "It's neat how it folds right into the bookcase."

"Thanks," Mary said. "My stepfather made— uh, designed it for me." They walked through the living room and into the tiny kitchen. "Peanut butter or tuna fish?" she asked, getting two plates from the cupboard above the sink.

"Let's make both," Elizabeth suggested, "and each have half."

They set to work and were soon seated at the table with their sandwiches, pickles, corn chips, and chocolate brownies. "Now, what did you want to talk to me about?" asked Mary.

"Well . . . nothing really. I just thought it would be fun to talk. You know . . . about things like your new stepfather and where you'll be moving to."

Mary was tired of telling lies about her stepfather. She was tired of talking about the wonderful new house. She wanted to tell someone the truth. "Elizabeth," she said, looking a little frightened, "that new house I told you about may not be all that terrific. I mean Jessica sort of got carried away, and I guess I let her. Besides, I don't think Tim has enough money to build a house like that."

"I know," Elizabeth said. "But the point is, it doesn't matter as long as you have two people who really care about you. Not counting all of us at school."

"Are you kidding?" Mary's lips trembled and her eyes filled with tears. "You should see the way the kids at school are treating me. Everyone's whispering and talking behind my back. I feel like I've got the plague or something." She paused, looking anxiously at Elizabeth. "Do you suppose it's because they know I didn't quite tell the truth?"

"Of course not, Mary. You're one of the most respected girls in our class. You've got tons of friends, and you're even a Unicorn."

"They're the worst of all!" Now tears started down Mary's cheeks. "You should see the way the whole club's been acting. I know they're all going to some big party without me. They're always whispering about clothes and presents, and every time I get near them, they change the subject."

Elizabeth was stunned. She and Jessica had been so sure that Mary didn't suspect a thing. Instead she was suspecting something totally wrong. "I'm sure you're just imagining it," she said.

"No. No, I'm not," Mary insisted, now crying hard. Between sobs she told Elizabeth how she'd been left out of things for weeks. How her mother and Tim rushed off after work and left her alone. "No one likes me, Elizabeth," she finished. "Not even my family. Tim's taking my mom away from me. I just know he is."

"How can you say that, Mary?" Elizabeth put her arm around her friend. "Why, your mother loves you a lot. I know she does."

"Then tell me why . . ." Mary asked, the tears still flowing, "why she hasn't even mentioned my birthday? Before Tim came, she promised we'd go to the beach for a birthday clambake. We were going to have a fire and music and everything." She put her head in her hands. "Now that he's here, it's all changed, and Mom's forgotten all about me."

Elizabeth didn't want to spoil the surprise party. But she needed to prove to Mary how much her family and friends cared. She couldn't let her go on thinking she was all alone. "I have to tell you something," Elizabeth said. "It was supposed to be a secret, but I think you should know."

Mary just kept crying. "Are you listening to me?" Elizabeth asked, but didn't wait for Mary to reply. "People *have* been whispering behind your back, Mary."

Mary lifted her head from her hands, her eyes shiny with tears. "I knew it," she said, choking. "Why, Elizabeth? Why would they do that?"

Elizabeth thought of Mary's mother calling all the kids in her class. She thought of Jessica hard at work on the silver bracelet. She thought of all the Unicorns making plans for the party. "Because we love you, Mary," she answered. "Because we all love you."

Ten

"What do you mean, everyone loves me?" Mary declared. "People who care about you don't whisper about you and leave you out of everything. I even heard Jessica talking about a special outfit everyone's wearing for some big Unicorn party I'm not even invited to!"

"That's *your* party, Mary."

Elizabeth saw the look of hope on her friend's face, and knew she'd made the right decision. It was time to set things straight.

"*My* party?" Mary asked.

"Yes. Your very own extra-special surprise birthday party."

Mary's tears stopped at once. She smiled and shook her head. "Oh," she said. "Here I was, mad at the Unicorns, and all along they've been planning this terrific surprise!"

"Well," admitted Elizabeth, "the Unicorns are in on everything, all right. But the people who started it all live right here."

Mary looked shocked. "You mean Mom and Tim?"

"You bet. It was *their* idea to give you a birthday party. That's why they haven't been home after school. They're getting everything ready." Elizabeth watched Mary's smile grow. "They've got a lot to do before your birthday. It's going to be a really big party. They've invited the Unicorns, and the whole class, too!"

"Wow!" Mary exclaimed. "I feel pretty silly. I've been so mad because they told me they were going to the harbor. I thought they were spending time on that awful boat."

"They are, silly," Elizabeth explained. "That's where the party's going to be! Won't it be great?"

Suddenly Mary's smile faded. A giant knot formed in her stomach. She couldn't believe her ears. Her mother and Tim had not only bought the most ridiculous boat in Sweet Valley, but now they'd invited her whole class to a party on it! Wait until her friends saw the lopsided old boat with its peeling paint and silly red smokestack! The day Tim had finally taken Mary to see it, she'd wished she could sink in between the planks on the dock. She was terrified that someone from school would see them.

It *was* good to know that her mother and Tim had meant well and that all their planning and scheming had included her. Still, it didn't change the fact that what was supposed to be a wonderful surprise was going to be the worst, most humiliating day of her life!

Elizabeth was beaming now, and Mary wondered what her friend's face would look like when she saw the ramshackle boat. Would anyone ever speak to her again? How would she ever explain all the ridiculous boasting she'd been doing?

But Elizabeth wasn't a Unicorn. Maybe she would understand how Mary had needed to create a terrific stepfather. Maybe she would like Mary even if her stepfather turned out to be an everyday carpenter instead of a world-famous architect. "Elizabeth, there's something I'd better tell you," Mary began. "You know that desk you liked in the living room? Tim didn't just design it; he *made* it."

Elizabeth grinned. "You don't have to sell me on Tim, Mary. I already think he's great." She popped the last bite of brownie into her mouth and glanced up at the clock. "Look at the time. We'd better hurry if we're going to get back in time."

Mary stood up. Maybe she wouldn't have to tell anyone about Tim after all. Not yet, anyway. Maybe, if the plan that was beginning to form in her mind worked, she wouldn't even have to go to her own birthday party! "OK," she told Elizabeth, leaving her plate in the sink. "Let's go."

On Friday, as she and her classmates were leaving math class, Mary put her plan into action. She saw Jessica and Ellen not far ahead in the hallway. "Ohhhh," she groaned. "My stomach!"

"Mary, what's the matter?" Jessica asked, rushing up to her.

"Ohhh," repeated Mary. She slumped where she stood in the hall. "Maybe I'd better go home." She held her stomach and leaned against the wall near the lockers.

"You—you just *can't* be sick!" Ellen declared. The next day was Mary's party.

"I just want to go home," Mary said feebly. She looked so pale and weak that Jessica and Ellen walked her right to the main office. One look at the thin, miserable Mary, and even the stern old secretary melted.

"Oh, dear," the secretary said softly. "You just sit right down here and I'll write you out an infirmary pass."

"Ohhh," Mary groaned. "Please, I need to go home." She sat in a chair by the secretary's desk and lowered her head. "Ohhh," she murmured quietly, as if she were trying to be very brave.

"But we do have our rules, dear," the secretary said gently. "You can only go home if the nurse gives you permission." She began writing on a form in front of her.

"I—I . . ." began Mary, holding her mouth now instead of her stomach. "I think I'm going to throw up!" She bent lower and rose off her chair, her hand still over her mouth.

"Oh, no!" the secretary exclaimed. "We can't have that. We can't have that. Here, dear, I'm calling your parents right now. Just hold on, for heaven's sake. Hold on!"

When Mary and her mother arrived home from

school, they found Tim getting ready for their regular afternoon trip to the harbor. "What's wrong?" he asked.

"I'm afraid Mary doesn't feel too well," Mrs. Wallace explained, giving Mary a hug.

"She does look a little pale," Tim said, helping Mary over to the couch.

Mary felt really awful by now. She felt guilty for pretending to be sick, but was too scared to stop. She couldn't face that birthday party; she just had to convince her mother to call it off. "Ohhh." She sighed, sitting with relief on the couch beside her mom. "I think I'm going to have to go to bed."

"Darling!" Her mother headed for the bathroom. "I'll get a thermometer and we'll take your temperature."

Mary thought that perhaps by now she really *might* be sick. Her head was throbbing and she felt pretty warm. Maybe she could miss her party without lying. "Ohhh," she repeated, feeling achy and tired.

"I'm glad tomorrow's Saturday," she said just before her mother put the thermometer in her mouth. "At least I can stay in bed without missing school."

Her mother looked worried. "I'm sure it's not all that serious," she said hopefully. "In fact," she announced when she'd waited a couple of minutes and pulled out the thermometer, "I'm sure you won't need to spend tomorrow in bed, young lady. You don't have a fever at all!" She smiled with relief and hugged Mary happily. "Now how about a cup of tea?"

"Maybe," Mary ventured, "I have something that doesn't come with a fever. Maybe we should go see Dr. Costa."

"I think we've bothered Dr. Costa enough with problems that are really our own to solve. Besides," she added happily, "I think after tomorrow a lot of those problems will be history."

But Mary knew that tomorrow wouldn't be the end of her problems. In fact, it would just be the beginning! What would the kids in school say when they saw that dilapidated tugboat? How could she possibly tell her mother and Tim that she was ashamed of their big surprise?

Eleven

◇

"It's just that she thinks we've forgotten her birthday," Tim told his wife after Mary had gone upstairs. "Everything will be fine tomorrow." He sat down beside her and slipped his guitar case from under the couch. "I've even written a song for the party."

He took out his guitar and sang a simple melody about love and trust. Each verse talked about building love like a house, adding room after room until the house had turned into a castle. The chorus was, "There's always room for more love."

"Oh, Tim," Mrs. Wallace said when he stopped singing, "that's lovely. It says just what we want to tell her."

"I hope she gets the message." Tim sighed. He picked up the guitar and strummed the melody quietly while his wife lay her head against his shoulder. A few minutes later, when Mary tiptoed to the top of the stairs, that's how she saw the two of them. Tim was playing, and her mother listening to him with a contented, dreamy expression on her face.

Tears started to form before she knew it. Stumbling back to her bed, Mary felt sorry for herself. Even though she wasn't really sick, she had expected her mother and Tim to be a little worried. Instead there they were, together again without her. *They aren't even thinking about me up here*, she fumed to herself. *Tim couldn't wait to get rid of me, so he could have Mom all to himself. He's playing some dumb love song for her, and he never even came up to see how I was. They just planned the party to keep from feeling guilty. They don't care after all!*

Alone in her room, Mary came to a desperate decision. It was clear her mother and Tim would be happier without her. And it was equally clear that tomorrow's party would make her the laughingstock of Sweet Valley Middle School. There was only one thing to do.

Quietly Mary made her way around her room. She opened some drawers and her closet, pulled out clothes and stuffed them into a little suitcase. Maybe she could spend a few days with the Altmans, the foster family that had wanted to adopt her before she'd found her mother. Then she decided she'd try to find her real father. If he didn't have a new family of his own, maybe he'd want her. Just her and nobody else.

Mary waited until the sky grew dark and she heard two sets of footsteps going up the stairs. As silent as a cat, she tiptoed down the stairs and into the kitchen. She opened the refrigerator as quietly as she could and took out a pear and an orange. Stuffing them into her pockets, she headed for the back door.

It was very dark outside. But anything was better than facing all those laughing kids on the boat tomorrow. They'd never let her forget the way she'd boasted about her "new" life. She closed the door tightly behind her. Then, at the bottom of the back steps, her foot landed on something that suddenly gave way beneath her.

"Ahhh!" The scream didn't even sound like her own voice. As she toppled headfirst onto the ground, Mary felt a sharp pain in her left arm. Then everything was quiet again. She looked up, dazed, to see the reflector on her bike wheel shining in the dark. She had tripped over her own bicycle!

The pain in her arm was terrible, and Mary could barely concentrate on anything else. Finally she pulled herself up onto the last step with her other arm and sat hunched over, wondering what to do. She couldn't think clearly. Her entire arm, from her elbow to her wrist, felt hot and was throbbing.

Her arm hurt too much to consider walking all the way to the Altmans' house. Thank goodness she hadn't woken anyone up. She'd just have to sneak in the way she'd snuck out. Slowly she reached for the door handle and turned it. But nothing happened! She tried again, this time turning it harder. Still the door refused to open. It must have locked when she closed it behind her. Hopelessly, Mary sank back onto the bottom step and started to cry.

She considered calling for her mother. But if she woke her up, there would be a lot of explaining to do. And, of course, her mother would tell Tim. He'd pretend to care, and the two of them would talk it over, without her. No. It would be better to sit here all night long. If only her arm didn't hurt so much. If only she could force herself not to feel the awful pain.

Just when she was sure she couldn't stand it any longer, the door behind her opened. It was Tim. It seemed he'd heard her fall and come to investigate. Silently, he stared first at Mary, then at the suitcase lying beside her. "Night rates *are* cheaper," he said, then started to help her to her feet.

"Ahhh!" Mary cried out in pain before Tim could even touch her arm. Now, looking serious, Tim knelt beside her in the dark and turned on the flashlight he'd brought with him.

"Let's take a look," he said gently, being careful not to touch the arm. The flashlight revealed a long red scrape along Mary's elbow. "It doesn't look bad," Tim said, "but you might have a sprain, too. I'll carry you." As carefully as if he were lifting a baby, he scooped Mary into his arms and carried her back into the kitchen. He walked into the living room and lay her down on the couch. "Now, you wait right here while I get your mom," he said.

"No!" Mary couldn't bear to have her mother find out she'd tried to run away. The whole idea seemed pretty ridiculous now that she was back in her own house. She didn't even *know* her real father. He could be living anywhere. And the way Tim stopped and came to sit down beside her now, made her trust him just the slightest bit. "Please," she begged. "Don't tell Mom."

Tim nodded silently. He went back outside and retrieved the suitcase, stuffing it in the kitchen broom closet. "All right," he told Mary, "it'll be our secret. But I sure would like to know what was so bad you couldn't wait until morning." He leaned over, adjusting an afghan so it covered her. "Can you tell me why you were running away?"

But Mary couldn't tell him. She couldn't explain that she was ashamed of him, of his job, and of his boat. Everything about him was so ordinary. And now as he listened to her so quietly, without telling her how silly she'd been, she was ashamed of herself, too. "I—I just wanted to leave," she told him, not daring to explain.

"Well, I had no idea things were that bad," he replied, shaking his head. "I want you to know, Mary, that if anyone leaves, it's going to be me." He looked very sad, then stood up and walked to the bottom of the stairs. "Andrea," he called. "Honey, come on down here."

True to his word, Tim didn't say a word about Mary's plans to run away. He told her mother that she'd tripped trying to put her bike away. "I guess she couldn't rest until it was safe in the garage," he said convincingly.

Mrs. Wallace bent over to examine her daughter's arm, and winced when she saw the scrape on her elbow. "Maybe we should take her to the hospital, Tim. It could be broken."

"Well, let's clean up that elbow right here first," Tim told her. "Then we'll see how Mary feels."

"All right." Mrs. Wallace left the room and came back a minute later with a moist towel. "Oh, you poor thing!" Mrs. Wallace soothed. "All for a silly old bike." She tried to rub Mary's arm, but Mary squealed in pain.

"Whoa, nurse!" Tim interrupted. "Let me try." Carefully, painstakingly, he cleaned out the scrape while he held Mary's hand. He was so gentle that it hardly hurt at all.

When Tim finished, he stood up. "I don't think it's anything to be worried about, but we should probably go to the hospital just to make sure. Do you feel up to the trip if I carry you?"

Mary nodded, then the three of them went to the car. Tim and Mrs. Wallace sat in the front seat, and Mary stretched out across the back seat. Her mother seemed really worried about her arm, and she kept turning to check on her. It was hard to stay calm when her mother was so nervous. "I *am* going to be all right, aren't I?" Mary asked Tim.

"Of course you are," Tim answered confidently. "You've probably just got a bad bruise." He pulled the car up to the emergency room doors, then stepped out and opened the car door.

Gently as ever, he helped Mary walk through the doorway and up to the nurse at the desk. Mrs. Wallace, teary-eyed, followed. "My daughter's been hurt," she told the nurse in a high-pitched voice that didn't sound at all like the one Mary was used to. "She needs attention right away!"

"It doesn't look like anything too serious," Tim added soothingly. "Probably a sprain, but we'd like to check for a fracture or break."

The nurse nodded and wrote a card up with the information that Tim gave her. Then, when another nurse arrived and called Mary's name, he helped carry her into the emergency room and placed her gently on a bed with a white curtain pulled back beside it. "The doctor will be right with you," the nurse announced, and bustled away.

"I'm not sure I believe that," said Mary's mother. "Look at all the patients they have here. Don't you think we should go and get a doctor before they forget we're here?"

"Mom, please!" Mary's arm was hurting badly now, and she just wanted to wait quietly. "I'm sure he'll be here as soon as he can."

"I think Mary's right, honey. Here, why don't you sit down, and I'll sing you both my hospital song."

"I didn't know you knew a hospital song," said Mary, grinning in spite of herself.

"I don't." Tim grinned back and winked at her. "I'm going to make it up as I go along." Then, in a funny whispery voice, he sang a ridiculous, silly song about being sick and being treated by absent-minded doctors who wrote prescriptions for all sorts of silly ailments. By the last verse Mary was giggling and her mother was smiling.

"Well," observed the doctor, drawing aside the curtain, "I don't usually get such happy patients in here!"

"That's because most of them don't have their own entertainment committee," said Mary, smiling gratefully at her stepfather. For a few minutes she'd forgotten all about the pain in her arm.

"Now we'll take a look at it." The doctor took Mary's hand and began to feel her arm very carefully. She winced in pain, but Tim put his hand on her shoulder, and she felt better.

"There's probably a small fracture here," announced the doctor. "We'll need to take some X rays to be sure. Then we'll put it in a cast for a while."

"Would you like us to leave, Doctor?" Tim asked.

"No!" Mary answered before the doctor did. "Please, don't go. I want you to stay." Suddenly she realized she wanted Tim to stay not only with her there, but at home, too. "I mean stay for good," she added, smiling.

"It won't be easy, you know." Tim looked serious but hopeful. "We've got to trust each other."

Mary knew just what he meant. She remembered what Dr. Costa had said about making room in her heart. She'd been so busy locking Tim out that she hadn't seen how kind and thoughtful he was. Without a word she reached out, and Tim gently took her hand and gave her a smile that told her he understood.

"That's OK," the doctor assured them. "Parents

are allowed to stay. Dad, just sit right down and keep your daughter company."

"But I'm not—"

"Shhh!" Mary commanded, putting a finger over her mouth. "If you don't tell, I won't."

Twelve

"I'm not hungry," Jessica announced, coming into the kitchen with a sigh. "In fact, I don't think I'll ever eat again!" It was Saturday morning, the day of Mary's party, the day she and Elizabeth and almost everyone in school had been waiting for. But Jessica was in a terrible mood.

"I know my French toast is a little burnt on one side," Mr. Wakefield admitted, "but I don't think it's *that* bad!"

"It's not that," Jessica wailed, sinking miserably into a seat beside her twin at the big oak table. "It's the mail!"

"Uh-oh," Steven said, reaching for his sixth slice of French toast, "don't tell me you still haven't heard from Tom Houston."

"Worse!" Jessica glared at her brother. "I *did* hear from him!"

"But that's wonderful dear," Mrs. Wakefield said. "Isn't that just what you were hoping for?"

Jessica waved the single sheet of paper she'd

torn from its envelope. "He says he can't come to our dance!"

"That's too bad, Jess," Elizabeth said. "But you should have known Tom Houston's much too busy and important to take time out to sing at a Unicorn party."

"Some great fan letter you wrote for me, Lizzie!" Jessica handed the paper to her sister. "Just look at the answer it got!"

"'Dear Fan,'" Elizabeth read aloud, "'As I'm sure you know, I would love to have the time to write a personal letter in response to each inquiry I receive. Unfortunately my busy schedule does not permit me to do this.'"

"Hmmph!" interrupted Jessica. "I have a busy schedule, too. But *I* took time out to write my own letter to *him*."

"'I hope,'" Elizabeth continued reading, "'that you will understand that, even though previous commitments will not allow me to attend your function, I wish your organization good luck in achieving its worthwhile aims. Sincerely, Tom Houston, Hollywood, California.'"

"I'll be the laughingstock of the whole club!" Jessica grabbed the letter back and stared at its neatly typed face with fury. "If it's the last thing I do, Tom Houston, I'm going to grow up to be a famous celebrity. And when you ask me to do something with you, I'm going to tell you that I've got too many 'previous commitments'!"

"Well," Mr. Wakefield remarked, "that's a pretty unique reason for wanting a career in entertainment!"

"I mean it," insisted Jessica, tearing up the letter and stuffing it into her empty juice glass. "I trusted Mr. Bigshot Houston, and he let me down. I told the whole club I could get him to sing for us. Now we're stuck with no entertainment and no money."

"I guess that puts an end to your 'worthwhile aims,'" Elizabeth observed sarcastically. One look at the furious expression on her twin's face, however, made her regret her teasing. "I'm sorry, Jess. Really I am. Come on up to my room," she said. "We'll try our outfits on for the party. Maybe that'll take your mind off Tom Houston."

Jessica brightened just the slightest bit. "It *will* be exciting, won't it?" she asked as the two girls headed upstairs. "I mean, this won't be some silly school party held during the daytime. We'll be on a glamorous yacht with *seventh* graders!"

"You have one particular seventh grader in mind, don't you?" Elizabeth took the blue skirt and blouse she'd chosen for the party out of her closet and laid it carefully across her bed.

"Well," Jessica told her, "when I put the finishing touches on his mother's charm, Bruce *did* thank me."

"Coming from Mr. Wonderful, that's quite a lot."

"Oh, Lizzie, you've never given Bruce Patman a chance. He's really very sweet. He even told me he might dance with me tonight if I promised to make another charm for his aunt."

"That's about the most conceited thing I ever heard of, Jessica!"

"Lizzie! I'm talking about Bruce Patman. That's a small price to pay. Besides," Jessica added slyly, "I've got to do something to impress the Unicorns now that I struck out with Tom."

"I wouldn't worry about that, Jess. I think everyone's so excited about Mary's party, they've forgotten all about your club dance."

"It will be *terrific*! The moonlight on the water, the music, the presents . . . Oh, no!" Jessica exclaimed in alarm.

"What is it? What's wrong?"

"I haven't finished Mary's bracelet. I brought some sandpaper home to work on it yesterday, and I forgot all about it." She dropped the earrings she'd been modeling for her twin back into the jewelry box on Elizabeth's dresser and set to work. "I want it to be the smoothest, most beautiful bracelet ever," she said as she polished the pretty silver band.

After the bracelet was finished, the twins went into town to do some last minute errands. When they arrived home it was just about time to get dressed for the party.

"Just think, Lizzie," Jessica said excitedly as she slipped on her purple sweatshirt. "In less than an hour we'll be on board the Wallaces' boat, dancing in the moonlight!"

"I know!" Elizabeth giggled, looking at herself in Jessica's mirror. "I can't wait!"

While Jessica and Elizabeth were dressing, Mary was getting ready to face the worst moment in her life. Alone in her room, she kept telling herself that she owed it to her mother and Tim to go through with the party. She couldn't bear to tell her mother that she was ashamed of the tugboat, especially now that she knew how sweet and kind Tim was.

The night before, as the three of them had driven home from the hospital, Mary had come to a difficult decision. She knew that they were a family now. And she knew that she would have to face up to all the lies she'd told her friends. She'd have to greet her classmates on board the broken-down old boat and put up with their nasty comments.

It's the least I can do for two people who've worked so hard to surprise me, Mary thought as she stared unhappily into her mirror. She knew how much her mother loved her. And after the previous night, she knew Tim really cared, too. She was going to have to return that love the best way she could—even if it meant losing every friend she had. Even if it meant being made fun of by every Unicorn in the whole club!

"Are you ready for your dinner out?" Tim asked, poking his head into the doorway of her bedroom. There was a new, relaxed tone in his voice now.

"Sure." Mary smiled, pretending not to know

about the surprise party. She had chosen a pretty green dress from her closet. It had big, loose sleeves which slipped easily over her cast.

"I have a present for you before we leave," Tim said, handing her the suitcase he'd hidden in the broom closet the night before. "I thought we'd keep it our little secret."

"Thanks." Mary took the bag and put it safely in her own closet.

"I meant what I said last night, you know, Mary." Tim sat down on her bed. "If anybody leaves, it's going to be me. I never want to come between you and your mother."

Mary felt so warm and happy, she almost forgot about the party. She sat beside Tim, looking up at him with an affectionate grin that made him smile right back. "And I meant what I said, too," she said softly. "I want you to stay—for good. I was running away to look for my real father, but last night I realized I already *have* one."

"In that case, why don't we make it official."

"What do you mean?"

"Your mother and I have spoken to the lawyers. They say that since your father has been contacted and has agreed to my adopting you, there's nothing to stop us from proceeding." He put an arm around Mary. "How would you like to be a Wallace?"

"I'd love it!" Mary felt all the pain and confusion of the last few months melt away. Her mother and Tim *did* want her! She was part of an honest-to-goodness family. An important part!

"Hey, you two," Mrs. Wallace announced from outside the door. "I'm hungry. Let's go!"

A few minutes later, when Tim turned the car off toward the harbor instead of continuing on to the restaurant they had told her about, Mary did her best to seem surprised. "Where are we going?" she asked.

"Last pier on the right," Tim announced proudly, pointing to where the tug was moored. There, looming in the twilight, was the big, newly painted boat with its giant smokestack.

But it certainly looked different! Tim and her mother had strung rows of colored lights all around the deck. Now the old boat looked like a wonderful place to have a party. Of course, it wasn't a sleek cabin cruiser or a racing boat, but it did look inviting as it bobbed and twinkled in the water. Then, as they got out of the car, she noticed the neat white lettering painted along the bow. "'S.S. Mary,'" she read out loud. They had named the boat after her!

"We couldn't think of a prettier name," Tim told her, his arms around her and her mother. Mary didn't know whether to laugh or cry. She was dreading the arrival of her friends, but she couldn't help feeling proud and grateful that her two favorite people had worked so hard to please her.

Mary's enthusiasm was short-lived, though. As soon as they all had boarded the tug and begun to look around, Janet Howell and three other eighth-grade Unicorns stepped out of a car beside the pier. Mary watched the girls put their hands above their eyes and survey the boat. "Look, it's a tugboat!" she heard Janet yell.

Bracing herself, Mary took a deep breath and got ready to face the worst. "You're right," she heard another girl squeal. "Isn't it great?"

Mary couldn't believe her ears, but as soon as they'd boarded the ramp and were standing beside her, her guests couldn't stop giggling and chattering. "Mary!" exclaimed Janet. "You never told us your boat was a tug! What a neat surprise! It's just about the cutest antique boat I've ever seen! It must have cost a fortune!"

"Well, actually, Janet," Mary began, determined to set the record straight, "it took a lot of work to fix it up. We're not exactly like lots of the families in Sweet Valley."

"You sure aren't," Bruce Patman observed, climbing on board to join them. "This is just about the greatest thing I've ever seen. I'll bet there's not another one like it for miles!"

"At least not another one as creaky or unreliable," Tim replied, laughing. "Would you like to see how she operates?"

"Would I? Hey, guys, hurry up!" Bruce waved to Rick Hunter and another classmate who was still standing on the dock. "This is going to be the neatest party ever!"

And it was. Everyone who saw the tug was instantly fascinated. Tim was kept busy giving Mary's friends tours of the engine room and showing them the tools he'd used to put the ship in working order.

And Mrs. Wallace got plenty of compliments for the way she had turned the old galley into a beautiful "sea cavern," complete with fish and anemones swimming in nets strung along the walls, and lovely flickering candles on the sailcloth tables.

If Mary had any doubts about how much her family or friends cared, they disappeared when she caught sight of the wonderful whale-shaped cake her mother had made and the heap of presents on the galley table. "Oh, my goodness," she gasped. "I've never seen anything so wonderful!"

With shouts of "Open mine first!" ringing in her ears, Mary began to work her way through the heap of gifts. She got lots of wonderful presents, including a purple T-shirt, an adorable stuffed panda, and a Johnny Buck album she'd been dying to own. But her favorite gift came in a yellow-checked package with a gold bow. She lifted the delicate silver bracelet from its tissue-paper nest. "It fits perfectly!" she exclaimed, modeling the pretty band, then hugging both twins.

The high point of the party came when Tim took out his guitar. "I have a special song I'd like to sing for a special person," he announced. As everyone gathered around him, he sang the song he'd written just for Mary. "Love takes time," he sang. "Love takes work. Brick by brick and stone by stone, we've built a house of love." His voice was deep and rich, and Mary watched the way all the Unicorns' eyes got misty when he smiled at them. "Love takes time," he sang again. "Love takes work, but now my love castle is finished, and my princess can move in." He finished his song, smiling right at Mary and making her feel like the most important person in the world!

Mary felt tears forming in her eyes, but she didn't even try to brush them away. Right in front of everyone she hugged her stepfather. "The boat is wonderful," she told him. "And so are my gifts. But you just gave me the best birthday present of all! I'll never forget tonight as long as I live, Tim." Again she felt the heavy, warm tears in her eyes. "I mean, Dad."

Before Tim could answer, he was surrounded by squealing, giggling Unicorns. "Oh, Mr. Wallace, you're as good a singer as Johnny Buck," Ellen Riteman sighed, her eyes shining.

"Don't be ridiculous!" Lila Fowler scolded, pushing her way to the front of the crowd. "You're a thousand times better than Johnny Buck, Mr. Wallace. Would you autograph my napkin?"

Tim laughed, and bent to sign all of the napkins that were instantly held out to him.

Suddenly Jessica knew her problems were over. She pushed her way through the crowd until she was next to Tim. "Do you by any chance know the theme from *Dream Chaser*?" she asked.

"Why, yes I do. I kind of like those songs. Want to hear some?"

Mary's stepfather didn't need to be asked twice. Everyone settled down to listen. After Tim performed the hits from the movie, Mary's friends called out requests.

"He knows all our favorite songs!" Ellen declared. "He's just too dreamy for words."

"I'm afraid my voice is about to give out," Tim finally told them. "What do you say we turn on the stereo and start our dance contest?"

"That's a great idea, Mr. Wallace," Jessica approved. "We've got to take good care of your voice." Her lashes were fluttering furiously, her wind-tossed hair and sweet smile lit by the string of lanterns above her. "That is, if you're going to perform at our Unicorn party next month."

The Unicorns started to jump up and down excitedly. "Oh, would you, Mr. Wallace? Would you? Please?"

Flattered and laughing, Tim Wallace agreed. "Well, I guess I could do one more performance. Would you like to have your party on the boat?"

The cheers, whistles, and wild applause that followed made the group's answer plain enough. "Now," Tim said, "let's see *you* perform!" He turned on the stereo. Music began to blare from the speakers he had rigged up on the deck. Two hours later, after they'd danced until their feet were sore and eaten six pizzas and the whole giant birthday cake, the tired, happy guests got ready to leave.

"Thanks for coming, everyone." Mary stood at the top of the ramp, saying good-bye. "I'm sorry I told you that Tim was a famous architect," she whispered to a group of Unicorns. "I just wanted you to like him so much, I sort of got carried away."

Janet, who was standing in front of the group, shook her head in amazement. "Mary," she said, "with a dad like that, you didn't have to make up anything. He's terrific just the way he is!"

"Yes," Mary admitted happily, "I guess he is." It felt wonderful not to have to lie and pretend anymore. "Thanks again," she told her friends. "Thanks for everything."

Jessica turned back to stare up at Mary on board the boat. "Boy, she sure looks happy!"

Elizabeth turned around, too. Even from far away she could see the smile on Mary's face as she stood waving from the deck, her arm around Tim. "I have to admit it, Jessica," she said. "You were right. Sometimes fairy tales really *do* come true!"

"Yep! It's just too bad Linda Lloyd missed the party tonight."

"That's right," Elizabeth said, remembering that Linda had to stay home to help her family pack for the movers.

"Linda missed the best party there's ever been, didn't she, Lizzie?"

"She sure did." Just then Elizabeth remembered Amy's suggestion to her about running for class president. "I guess that means it's time to elect a new president," she said. Maybe she would run after all.

"And I hope it'll be me!" Jessica declared. "I've always wanted to run for office. Do you think I could do it?"

Oh, no, thought Elizabeth. If she wanted to be

elected class president, she'd have to run against her own twin sister!

Will Elizabeth and Jessica run against each other for class president? Find out in Sweet Valley Twins 14, **TUG OF WAR.**

We hope you enjoyed reading this book. All the titles currently available in the Sweet Valley Twins series are listed at the front of the book. They are all available at your local bookshop or newsagent, though should you find any difficulty in obtaining the books you would like, you can order direct from the publisher, at the address below. Also, if you would like to know more about the series, or would simply like to tell us what you think of the series, write to:

Kim Prior,
Sweet Valley Twins
Transworld Publishers Ltd.
61–63 Uxbridge Road
Ealing
London W5 5SA

To order books, please list the title(s) you would like, and send together with a cheque or postal order made payable to TRANSWORLD PUBLISHERS LTD. Please allow the cost of the book(s) plus postage and packing charges as follows:

All orders up to a total of £5.00   50p
All orders in excess of £5.00   Free

Please note that payment must be made in pounds sterling; other currencies are unacceptable.

(The above applies to readers in the UK and Republic of Ireland only)

If you live in Australia or New Zealand and would like more information about the series, please write to:

Sally Porter
Sweet Valley Twins
Transworld Publishers (Aust) Pty. Ltd.
15–23 Helles Avenue
Moorebank
N.S.W. 2170
AUSTRALIA

Kiri Martin
Sweet Valley Twins
c/o Corgi and Bantam Books New Zealand
Cnr. Moselle and Waipareira Avenues
Henderson
Auckland
NEW ZEALAND

Created by FRANCINE PASCAL

Jessica and Elizabeth Wakefield have had lots of adventures in *Sweet Valley High* and *Sweet Valley Twins* . . .

Now read about the twins at age seven! All the fun that comes with being seven is part of *Sweet Valley Kids*. Read them all!

1. SURPRISE! SURPRISE!
2. RUNAWAY HAMSTER
3. THE TWINS' MYSTERY TEACHER
4. ELIZABETH'S VALENTINE
5. JESSICA'S CAT TRICK
6. LILA'S SECRET
7. JESSICA'S BIG MISTAKE
8. JESSICA'S ZOO ADVENTURE
9. ELIZABETH'S SUPER-SELLING LEMONADE
10. THE TWINS AND THE WILD WEST
11. CRYBABY LOIS
12. SWEET VALLEY TRICK OR TREAT
13. STARRING WINSTON EGBERT
14. JESSICA THE BABYSITTER
15. FEARLESS ELIZABETH

SWEET VALLEY KIDS SUPER SNOOPERS

1. THE CASE OF THE SECRET SANTA